Mischief Done

Mischief Done

J.A. O'Brien

ROBERT HALE · LONDON

© J.A. O'Brien 2012
First published in Great Britain 2012

ISBN 978-0-7198-0500-4

Robert Hale Limited
Clerkenwell House
Clerkenwell Green
London EC1R 0HT

www.halebooks.com

2 4 6 8 10 9 7 5 3 1

Typeset in 11½/16pt New Century Schoolbook
by Derek Doyle & Associates, Shaw Heath
Printed in Great Britain by the
MPG Books Group, Bodmin and King's Lynn

PROLOGUE

'Bless me Father, for I have sinned.' The Catholic priest waited patiently while the dying man got his breath to continue his confession. The man had collapsed in the street, struck down by a stroke. 'It's been a long time, Father.' The priest made consoling noises. 'And I've sinned gravely.' More consoling noises. He hated being a hospital chaplain; hated the constant misery; the constant reminders of how frail one's hold on life was. He dreamed of a country parish. However, nearing retirement, he knew that he would never have his wish fulfilled. Forty years he had been a priest, one city parish after another, each grottier than the one before. A quiet country parish would not have been too much to ask for, after so many years of loyal and dedicated service.

The man's chest began to heave. The presence of death was all around now.

The penitent beckoned to the priest urgently. The priest leaned closer to hear the man's whisperings, repulsed by the dying man's foul breath. . . .

CHAPTER ONE

Andy Lukeson looked with weary resignation at the pile of junk mail on his doormat, amazed at how much had accumulated in the couple of days leave he had taken after the Helen Blake murder investigation.* The case had been led by him, deputizing for DI Jack Porter while he was on sick leave – leave which had since become retirement. He had been offered Porter's vacancy, but had refused the offer. Foolishly or not, Lukeson was not yet sure.

Time alone would tell.

Angry that post he did not want should be foisted on him, he grabbed the lot, balled it up and binned it. It was only when he was turning away that he spotted a private letter amongst the junk. He retrieved it from the bin, and was instantly elated on recognizing the slanted style of DI Sally Speckle's handwriting. Speckle had not been seen or heard of since she had opted out six weeks ago before her head, as she had expected, went on the chopping block – a victim of pure chance that had left her career hanging in the balance.

* See *Murder In Mind*.

Though she had not been directly involved, it had been fallout from the Blake murder which had precipitated Speckle's departure on extended leave and possible eventual resignation.

'There was no talking her out of it, Andy,' had been Chief Superintendent Frank 'Sermon' Doyle's opinion, when challenged by Lukeson.

'You just let her walk out,' Lukeson had accused his superior.

'Mind your tone of voice, laddie. Sally Speckle is a grown woman who's entitled to do as she pleases. She had her mind made up. There was nothing I could say or do that would make her change it, try as I might.'

Unheeding of the warning in Doyle's tone of voice, he had retorted tetchily, 'There must have been something you could have done.'

'Sally asked me if it was likely that she would be disciplined. I gave her an honest answer. I told her that sacrifice would likely be demanded. And that sacrifice would probably be her head on a plate. But I also told her that I would stand by her, and I bloody well would have.

'It's not often coppers like Speckle come down the line. Who'd have thought that a graddie would become one of Loston's finest.'

Doyle, a traditionalist, but not the died-in-the-wool variety, admitted: 'Frankly, I'd never have thought it could happen. So I don't need to get a thick ear from you, Lukeson. I've already got one from Assistant Chief Constable Alice Mulgrave. Speckle made quite an impression on the ACC. If she wants to walk back in here, her old job will be waiting. But she hasn't got forever to make up her mind.'

Lukeson opened the letter from Sally Speckle. It read:

Hello Andy,
It's difficult to know where to begin, but I suppose I'll start by asking you how you are. Good, I hope. I left without saying well done on the great success of your first solo murder investigation. I bet all the talk has been about the *graddie* who cocked up big time with, of course, the inevitable: I told you so. Manna from heaven for the trads, eh. . . .

'Running away didn't help, Sally,' Lukeson mumbled. 'Never had you figured for a quitter.' His guilt was immediate. Easy for him to say. But, facing the same scenario as Sally Speckle had, he wondered how he might have reacted. Maybe not much differently, he thought.

. . . God I must sound sorry for myself. Look, letter writing was never my forte so I'll stop right here, Andy. If you want to chat, here's my phone number. It's an Irish number. . . .

Lukeson recalled Speckle's fondness for wide open spaces, like the Bear, a Pennisula in West Cork.

. . . Well, that's it. Bye, Andy.

'Bye, Andy,' echoed inside Lukeson's head. It sounded so . . . final.

PS. You were an idiot not to have taken Jack Porter's job. You'd have made a very good DI. Maybe not as

9

brilliant as me, hah hah. But then someone like me comes down the line only once in a while. Right?

'Too bloody right, ma'am,' he said. 'Too bloody right!'

There was no address on the letter, which probably meant that she did not want to be found. Had there been an address, he'd be on his way to Ireland right now to bring her back. He went to the phone, and was about to pick it up to call Speckle when it rang. He looked at it sourly. The caller display told him that it was Chief Superintendent Frank 'Sermon' Doyle.

'Just in the bloody door,' he groaned, picking up the phone.

'Lukeson?'

'Who else, sir,' Lukeson sighed.

'Don't be a smartarse, Sergeant,' Doyle growled. 'You were supposed to be back yesterday.'

'I did have that optional extra day's leave coming, sir.'

'All right. So you did. But now that you're back, my office in twenty minutes.'

As usual, when Doyle was of a mind not to answer any questions, he hung up.

'No need to break the bloody door down,' Doyle shouted, in response to Andy Lukeson's hefty knock fifteen minutes later. 'Turn the bloody handle, it's open.'

Entering, Lukeson could not resist quipping: 'I might have been the Chief Constable, sir.'

'No, you couldn't, Lukeson. Coppers of such lofty rank don't think it neccessary to knock. They just assume that they have licence to roam free. Sit.'

Lukeson sat on the chair facing Doyle squarely. The

chair was a set piece in the Chief Super's office which, in all the years he'd been coming and going, had never moved a single inch. Lukeson wondered if the chair was nailed to the floor. Having had several hundred bottoms (if not thousands) of every shape, size and weight on it, the upholstery had dipped in the middle, making the seat uncomfortable – unless one's posterior fitted perfectly into the dimensions of the dip, in which case it could be quite cozy . . . not that anyone wanted to linger for too long. The chair had, in it's time, soaked up quite an amount of perspiration, to which he had made his own contribution from time to time.

Doyle was standing at the window looking out on the street. On Lukeson's way into the station an ambulance had sped away carrying a man who had collapsed outside the station. Regaining his seat, Doyle enunciated the reason for Lukeson's summoning. 'I want you to find Miranda Watts, Andy.'

The abduction of the nine year old, the only child of Sarah Watts, former catwalk queen, now high profile businesswoman and Danny Marlaux the doyen of horse trainers, had been big news for days.

'Me? I'm a detective sergeant, sir.'

'And your point is?'

'Well, it should be a DI at least. If not a DCI that would head up the investigation.'

'DI Allen had been assigned, before he went and slipped on dog do-do and broke his ankle.'

'Bad luck, that.'

'Particularly when he was favourite to win the national Police Officers dance competition and bring the trophy to Loston.' Doyle, himself no slouch on the dance floor, took a

11

keen interest in the competition. 'Dances the tango like a native.' He groaned. 'Or at least he did.'

The wonder was, that Allen, a tall, slow-moving, sometimes positively awkward man, turned into a natural when he set foot on a dance floor and became a torrid and passionate dancer.

'I'm sorry to hear about DI Allen's accident, but I'd respectfully point out that there are other Detective Inspectors, sir.'

'Tight budgets. Three on the sick. Two vacant posts, one, Jack Porter's, which you could have filled. And Sally Speckle's. In a nutshell, that leaves you.'

DS Andy Lukeson was not flattered that he was chosen by default. But if his reaction showed on his face, which he felt it must have, CS Doyle chose to ignore it.

'I've already refused DI Porter's vacancy, sir,' Lukeson needlessly reminded his superior. 'I'm not interested at present in being an Acting DI again.'

'It may have slipped your notice, Sergeant,' Doyle said curtly, 'That the police force is not a democracy. It's an organization based on obeying orders. And I've just given you one.' Assuming obedience, Doyle pressed on: 'The preliminaries are already in train. Door-to-door. Reconstruction of crime scene. Appeal. Woods. Drains. Ditches. Waste ground. Derelict buildings. Roadblocks. Airports. Seaports. Railway stations. Three days of nothing.' he said, exasperated.

'Where was the child abducted?'

'A place called Cherrytree Lane. On her way home from school.'

'Witnesses?'

'None.'

'Then how can we be sure that she was actually abducted?'

'Her schoolbag and one very expensive shoe, verified by Sarah Watts as belonging to her daughter. As I've said, no witnesses. But a green van or perhaps a jeep, described as pretty clapped out, was seen entering Cherrytree Lane about the time we believe the abduction took place.'

'Registration?'

Doyle shook his head.

'Name on the van?'

'No. It was just a green van.'

'Or jeep,' Lukeson said. 'Easy to spot the difference, wouldn't you say, sir?'

'Not when you're driving a bus and another vehicle cuts across you. I reckon you'd be kept busy doing what you'd have to do to avoid an accident. The bus driver reported the incident to Traffic at the time because an elderly passenger fell off her seat when he swerved. Traffic alerted squaddies in the area, but no sign of the vehicle.

'It was only when Sarah Watts reported her daughter missing that the penny dropped.'

'The fact is then, that this van might or might not be important.'

'Suspicious, though,' Doyle said.

'Cherrytree Lane?'

'It borders Brate Hall. Long gone, the Brates. Now owned by a woman called Letty Hosford. Horsey set type.' Doyle sighed. 'Pity.'

'What is?'

'She's closed the Hall to visitors. Deprived a lot of people from making a few quid when the busloads of tourists dried up.'

13

'Does Cherrytree Lane lead to the Watts house?'

'Yes. Another country pile. Not far beyond Brate Hall.'

'How long before she was reported missing?'

'Four hours, give or take.'

'How far is her home from the school?'

'Not far. Fifteen minutes, thereabouts.'

'A nine year old girl. Almost on her own doorstep. Missing for four hours and—'

'There was no one at home. Sarah Watts, the former model and now business high-flyer, was away on business. You've heard of her?'

Yes, Lukeson had heard of her. In fact his best mate at school, one Danny Marlaux, horse trainer extraordinaire had, up to a year ago, been Sarah Watts's hubby. 'Yes, sir. I know of her.'

'Extraordinary woman,' Doyle said admiringly. 'Lost her modelling career to a bout of tubercolosis, then picked herself up and started a chain of jewellery shops, when most, on losing out on a glittering career, would have folded their tent and slunk away to obscurity and self-pity.'

When CS Frank 'Sermon' Doyle had done with admiration, he went on:

'There was a woman who would normally have been at the house, but she was visiting a sick relative, hence the delay in reporting the girl missing.' Frank Doyle's face took on a look of disapproval. 'There's a man, a live-in . . . *friend* of Watts. . . .'

'Her lover?'

'Don't mince your words, do you, Lukeson,' Doyle grunted.

'I've always found that being direct saves time, sir.'

'Watts gave him the heave-ho last week.'

14

'Name?'

'Bennett. Simon Bennett.'

'Form?'

'None.'

'Or nothing known,' Lukeson said. 'What's Bennett got to say for himself?'

'We'll ask him when we find him.'

'Done a runner, has he?'

'Just let's say that for now he's not in Loston or its immediate environs.'

'Lovers' tiff, was it, sir?'

'Lovers don't tiff nowadays. That, laddie, was for more genteel times. Now they have a right old set to and storm off when every bit of crockery and most of the windows have been smashed.'

'How terribly working class,' Lukeson said, tongue in cheek. Doyle shot him the kind of look he might have given something nasty on the sole of his shoe. 'Did Mr Bennett get redundancy? Or perhaps a . . . *service* gratuity?'

'Rehearsing to become a stand-up, are you, Lukeson?'

'His pay-off, or lack of, could be very relevent, sir. Maybe, nose out of joint, with only the lining in his pockets, Bennett decided to even the score with Watts by abducting her daughter?'

'Three days. No ransom demand. If it was money Bennett wanted, why would he delay?'

'Raise anxiety to new heights? He might reason that the more rattled Sarah Watts became, the more she'd be prepared to part with. Watts under surveillance, is she? Phones being monitored?'

'It might have missed your notice, Lukeson. But when you're not here, Loston nick functions quite well without you. Of course she's under surveillance. And of course the bloody phones are being monitored. Come up to scratch, do we, Sergeant?'

'Bennett's background, sir?'

'Posh. A daddy with oodles. Boarding school. Cambridge. A London banker.'

'He'll be used to holding people to ransom then.' Doyle did not appreciate the witticism. 'How come he ended up a gigolo?'

'Nice work, if you can get it, I suppose.' Doyle's shoulder's slumped. 'It's been three days, Andy. I'm of a mind to think that it isn't a money thing. Ransom is understandable. Thug needs money. Abducts girl. Thug gets money. Purely business. But if it's not money, then that leaves a motive more sinister.'

'There might be another reason, sir.' Doyle raised a quizzical eyebrow. 'Anything to suggest that Bennett and Miranda Watts were . . . *close?*'

'They got on well with each other, is how Sarah Watts described it to DI Allen. What're you thinking, Andy?'

'Marriage on the rocks. Danny Marlaux gone. Bennett became a surrogate father. . . ?'

'Go on.'

'Bennett gets the boot. Miranda goes with him. Maybe because she really wanted to. Or maybe to punish her mother for giving him his marching orders. There's also the possibility that Miranda Watts became infatuated with Bennett.'

'Infatuated? She's nine years old.'

'Nine, these days, isn't what nine was, even not long ago. There's been an incessant drive through the media, films, telly, the internet and advertizing to sexualize

16

children. It's an evil bloody carry on to make money and should be stopped in its tracks. Anything known about Bennett's background? Peculiarities? Mental problems?'

'Nothing to hand.'

'Did Sarah Watts say why she turfed Bennett out?'

'Just tired of him apparently. Seems she likes change. Is it any wonder the world's in the bloody mess it's in. Nothing lasts anymore.'

'What if Sarah Watts saw or sensed something that wasn't right?'

'She'd have said.'

'She'd have introduced this possible danger into her daughter's life. Might not be that easy an admission to make. Sarah Watts would not be the first to move the problem along rather than out it.'

'Progress to date,' Doyle handed over a thin file, and groaned: 'Or, more correctly, lack of. Read. Then get along to Watts.'

Lukeson would get along to Watts first, and read later, preferring to come fresh to the interview rather than conditioned by another officer's notes and opinions. Having spoken to Sarah Watts, he reckoned that he'd be in a better position to evaluate Allen's work so far. He knew from experience that preliminary interviews with those close to the victim fell into the softly softly category. Too much emotion involved.

'Bennett aside,' Doyle said. 'My money is on a much more likely prospect. A man called Curly. . . .'

'Do you do murders?'

'Pardon, madam,' WPC Anne Fenning queried.

'I want to speak to someone who does murders,' the

woman insisted, in a voice barely above a whisper.

Fenning had a mental image of an elderly woman, hand cupping the mouthpiece, looking over her shoulder.

'Yes,' Fenning said, wisely, fearing that had she told her that she would put her on to a senior officer she would hang up.

'Oh, good,' she said, relieved. 'Because you see, I've seen a murder.'

'Really?' Sounding unintentionally patronizing, Fenning winced.

'You don't believe me!'

'Yes, I do.' Even more patronizing. 'Where did you see this murder?'

'I'm not sure I should bother speaking to you,' the woman said huffily. Fenning waited. There was nothing else she could say or do but wait for the caller to make the next move. Procedure ordained that she get the woman's name and the number she was calling from. However, Fenning judged that any attempt on her part to follow procedure would almost certainly backfire. She crossed her fingers under the desk, and prayed that she would not hang up. 'Thatcher's Lot,' the woman finally said.

Thatcher's Lot,* Fenning thought, recalling an earlier case.

'A child,' the woman said. 'A little girl.'

Miranda Watts came instantly to mind.

'When was this?'

'Half an hour ago at most. He just dumped her body. Threw her away like rubbish. Most cruel, don't you think?'

'Indeed,' Fenning agreed, wondering if now was the right

---

* See *Old Bones*.

time to ask the woman her name and location. Not just yet, she decided. 'Did you actually see this man—'

'Well, not then and there. He obviously had murdered her somewhere else and was then disposing of the b—'

'Hilly!'

Another woman's voice. Distant. Strident. Commanding.

'Have to go,' the woman said breathlessly.

'Hilly!!!'

The woman again. Now much closer.

'Could I have your name and phone number, please?' Fenning asked desperately.

'Oh, no. She wouldn't like that. Oh, no. Not one little bit. I'm not supposed to use the phone, you see.'

'It would help us greatly if—'

'Hilly. You're not on the phone, are you?'

The woman was closer still. Fenning could hear footsteps.

'Must go.'

The line went dead.

'Shit!' Fenning swore.

She should have tried to have the call traced. But she had stupidly thought at first that she was dealing with a dotty old dear, a type not unknown to police. She might still be. She could hope. At least until a search of Thatcher's Lot was completed. But somehow, Anne Fenning had an overwhelmingly sinking feeling that it would be as the woman had said.

'Samuel Curly?'

'I'm impressed, Andy,' Doyle said. 'You know of him.'

'It would be hard not to. Any time DC Clive Bailey gets

19

you cornered for a minute. . . .'

'Ah, yes. Bailey. An officer to whom young Katherine Stockton has a lot to be grateful for. If he hadn't found her, Lord knows what might have happened to her.'

'That's what Bailey tells everyone he meets. Even if he meets them ten times a day,' Lukeson groaned.

'We were fortunate that DC Bailey decided to transfer to Loston from Brigham. He's become quite a star in the Training Division.'

Fortunate my bum, Lukeson thought. Brigham were glad to see the back of DC Clive Bailey.

'Fits the profile, does he, sir, Curly?' Then, more daringly: 'Poorly educated and working class.'

'Don't wave the bloody red flag at me, Lukeson,' Doyle barked. 'Curly was convicted of Stockton's abduction. Why go haring about the place when the obvious is staring you in the face.'

'In my experience, sir. The obvious has often been the trap into which the plods fall.'

'And sometimes, plods, by their gregarious nature want to play Sherlock Holmes, preferring to be hailed as clever than pedestrian. There's no glory in the unspectacular, eh.'

Lukeson apologized. He had been unfair to Doyle, whose track record was one of fairness.

'Katherine Stockton was about the same age, not unlike Miranda Watts in appearance, and also of a similar social background,' the CS emphasized.

To which, Lukeson countered:

'Having only got out of prison a couple of days before Miranda Watts went missing, would Curly have had time to plan her abduction? And he'd know that the plods would be on his doorstep before he could blink when

Miranda Watts vanished.'

'They were.'

'And?'

'Not at home. And the last time he was seen was by his upstairs neighbour, a couple of hours before Miranda Watts went missing. This neighbour says that Curly was preoccupied, quote, *off in a world of his own.*'

'Preoccupied? I'm often preoccupied trying to decide between fish and chips or pizza.'

'Being in a world of his own could mean that Curly was thinking about what he was on the verge of doing,' Doyle said. 'As for not having had time to plan, Stockton's abduction had all the hallmarks of being spur-of-the-moment as Watts may well have been also. And having been banged up for so long, the temptation for Curly to act might have been overwhelming.'

Lukeson recognized the soundness of his superior's reasoning. But that ran counter to Samuel Curly's persistent protestations of his innocence of Katherine Stockton's abduction, in fact even to the point of impeding his release from prison by refusing to acknowledge his crime and to express remorse for it.

Frustrated, Doyle barked, 'Samuel Curly's a convicted child abductor, Lukeson!'

Not ready to yield, Lukeson argued: 'The evidence against him was thin and circumstantial. But what there was, was very cleverly presented by the prosecution and weakly defended, at a time when the media was full of the trial in Manchester of a serial child molestor who had turned child killer.

'So might it not be possible that in Curly's case, the jury returned a verdict based on emotion rather than evidence?'

'You're a copper, Lukeson,' Doyle growled. 'Not a drum banger for some loony *there's good in everyone* brigade! Facts, man. Curly, a tried and convicted child abductor gets out of prsion. Another child, very similar to his first victim goes missing. That, in my book, makes Samuel Curly the prime suspect. So let's run him to ground!'

'Was his flat searched?'

'Of course it bloody was! Clean as the proverbial whistle.'

'People who obsess about kids carry baggage, sir. Was there anything in Curly's flat to point to his standing as a sexual predator?'

Doyle shook his head, annoyed. 'Look, Andy. The obvious is a good starting point.'

'Can't argue with that, sir,' Lukeson said.

'That makes a change,' Doyle grunted. 'You can be a thorny one, Lukeson.' Pot calling the kettle black, Lukeson thought. But there was no way he was going to point out the obvious. 'Well, come on, laddie,' the CS urged, in response to Lukeson's pensive mood. 'Out with it.'

'If Curly was innocent last time round,' Doyle groaned, but Lukeson would not be put off. 'He might simply have panicked and gone to ground. It's easy to understand why he might.' Doyle pulled a face that Lukeson was not sure how to interpret. He did not comment for or against Lukeson's rumination. 'As I recall, there was nothing sexual in Katherine Stockton's abduction?'

'The bugger hadn't got round to it, I expect,' Doyle stated sourly. Doyle's was a commonly held view. 'Drove her to the caravan in which Clive Bailey found her, a prisoner for three days. Might have lost his bottle. Maybe he was somehow side-tracked. Or maybe Curly was waiting for police activity to quieten down. Perhaps that's what he's doing right now. No ransom demand for Watts. None for Stockton either. Another common link between Watts and Stockton. Overall, I believe Curly is our man.'

'I agree that it stacks up against Curly,' Lukeson said.

'Good,' Doyle grunted, figuring that he had won the argument.

'But a child molester, in heat, is driven. Unheeding of risk.'

Exasperated by Lukeson's return to a subject which Doyle reckoned he had closed, he picked up a folder on his desk. 'Curly's file. I like to see my facts in print rather than on a bloody screen.' He slid the file across the glistening, polished desk, forcing Lukeson to act quickly to stop it from ending up on the floor, a mess needing to be put back in order. 'Nothing more than a crime against a child that gets up my nose, Andy.'

'Understandable, sir. If Watts's abductor was of a mind to clear out immediately, he'd have gone a considerable distance in any one of a hundred directions before the abduction was reported. He could even have fled the country.'

'You can be a depressing sod sometimes, Lukeson,' Doyle grunted. 'But of course you're right. So we can only hope that Miranda Watts's abductor is a homebird. Curly didn't go far the last time, so maybe he's repeating the pattern, eh. And don't remind me again, however diplomatically, that I'm jumping to the obvious,' he barked in response to Lukeson's raised right eyebrow.

'What if the abductor was aware, on the day, of Watts's domestic circumstances, and knew that time was on his side. Bring us back to Bennett, perhaps?'

23

'Good point,' Doyle complimented. 'But Bennett was out of the picture, kicked out by Sarah Watts.'

'He might have been in contact with Miranda. But, having been on the inside track for a time, it might not have been too difficult, possibly through a common friend of his and Sarah Watts, to acquire the information he needed.'

Doyle thought about what Lukeson had said, but did not favour or reject his ponderings. 'Something else . . .' Doyle picked up a folder and a disc. 'Transcription and recording of Sarah Watts's 999 call. She mentions a woman called Sylvia Planter. A psychic. Spiritualist. Medium. Whatever. Anyway, a couple of nights before Miranda Watts disappeared, at a party at the Watts's house, they indulged in a bit of hocus-pocus during which this Planter woman told Watts that there was danger around. What she termed *imminent* danger.'

Lukeson read through the typescript. He was struck by its matter-of-fact style, which he thought odd. 'It's very precise and concise, isn't it. Not what you'd expect from a distraught woman. 999 calls are usually panicky. This is a woman reporting her nine year old daughter missing. She'd be tense. Anxious. Yet, taking this transcription as an indication of her mood, she seems to have been very much in control.'

'Sarah Watts is a very successful businesswoman. Focus. Control. Part and parcel of that kind of woman.' Doyle studied Lukeson. 'You're not seeing anything sinister, are you?'

DS Andy Lukeson shrugged. 'Women have harmed their children before.'

'Indulging your flight of fancy, what motive might

Sarah Watts have for harming her only child?'

Andy Lukeson hunched his shoulders. 'If there is one, hopefully it'll be quickly established, sir.'

'Of course you're right, as the jargon of the day would have it, to think outside the box. But I think you shouldn't give the idea too much of your time, Lukeson. Nothing's come of the telly appeal. People don't want to get involved anymore. But they expect the police to pull rabbits out of a hat! And grumble and groan when they can't.'

Doyle had voiced the classic copper's gripe.

'And who could blame them,' he said with weary resignation. 'Crime and criminals have become ruthless and vicious, often resulting in long-term trouble for those who dare to come forward. And the inconsequential nature of sentences handed down, don't come any way near approaching a deterrent. Arrangements are being made for a second appeal by Sarah Watts.'

He grabbed the papers he had been working on when Lukeson had arrived and waved them about like a communist agitator rousing the mob.

'Bloody budget.' CS Frank 'Sermon' Doyle, who's responsibilities included keeping tabs on the cost of running Loston nick, had acquired his nickname by virtue of his rants about overtime. 'The dreaded axe has fallen. The next three months, until the new budget kicks in, we'll have to make do with what we've got, which isn't a lot.'

That, thought Andy Lukeson, probably explained why he had been railroaded. Had he had any thoughts about being flattered, they were now truly binned.

'I've had a path worn to my door by those who want Speckle declared gone, who reckon that they should get her job. And if there's no one banging the door down, ACC Alice Mulgrave is on the blower reminding me that there's a moratorium on everything except drawing breath, and only that if it doesn't cost. But at the moment, the budget restrictions favour Speckle. If they had not come, the pressure to fill her job would probably have been unstoppable.

'It beats me, how do the people who make these decisions reckon we can provide decent policing to the public with less and less in the kitty in real terms year on year.'

Lukeson had been again about to reiterate his lack of willingless to take on another case as an Acting DI. Having filled in against Jack Porter's vacancy in the Helen Blake murder he had suffered, thinking that Blake's killer would elude him. And other than his own misgivings, there was also the sometimes open hostility towards him by officers who deemed themselves better qualified. Once he had caught Helen Blake's killer, it was assumed when Jack Porter called it a day that he'd step into his shoes, and he supposed it was what he himself had expected. However when he was offered Porter's vacancy, he had found himself oddly unenthusiastic about taking it. Since then, there were times he thought he should have. And there were times when he reckoned that he had made the right decision, feeling that he was a natural Watson to someone else's Holmes. Or perhaps a Hastings to someone else's Poirot. Whatever, he had settled in nicely again to being a detective sergeant. And now this.

'You'll head up Speckle's old team, Andy,' CS Doyle informed him.

Stepping into Sally Speckle's shoes made a difference. All the difference. It meant that while he was acting against her vacancy, it would not be filled. Of course there was one way in which it might be filled, a small voice inside his head reminded him, and that was if he dead-ended and it became necessary to bring fresh thinking to find Miranda Watts.

The misgivings he had suffered in the hunt for Helen Blake's killer came back to haunt him.

'Cat got your tongue?' Doyle grunted.

Lukeson had not realized how long he had given over to his thoughts. 'If I'm keeping Sally Speckle's chair warm until she comes back, that's fine with me, sir. In no time at all the furore that drove her away will die down and she'll be back.'

'It might not be as easy as that, Andy,' Doyle confided companionably. 'Walking back in is never as easy as walking out. Time isn't on her side. We can't keep the door open for much longer. Anyway, it would be unfair to those waiting in the wings.'

He sighed heavily.

'I want to see Speckle back, as much as you do, but it grows more difficult by the day. One thing Speckle has going for her is Alice Mulgrave's support. But even an assistant chief constable can't hold out forever.

'Why the hell didn't you take Jack Porter's job when he packed in, Andy. You could have shot up the greasy pole of promotion, laddie, after your success in your first solo murder inquiry.'

'I put the cuffs on the killer, true enough,' Lukeson said. 'But would I have, if Sally Speckle hadn't pointed the way?'

'You'd have got there,' Doyle said with genuine

confidence. 'Might have taken a bit longer, but you'd have nabbed Blake's killer. Refusing Porter's job, you could have shot your bolt, you know. There's the distinct danger that, in football parlance, you'll spend the rest of your career coming off the bench but never making the first team.'

'The subs as well as the stars go to make up a team, sir.'

'Very philosophical, I'm sure. But no bloody good when it comes to pension! All that counts then is final pay.'

Lukeson had to concede that Frank Doyle's reasoning had a lot going for it, and as he drew nearer to his pension he'd likely regret his impulsive refusal of promotion.

'Hasn't been in touch, has she?' Doyle enquired, studying Lukeson closely.

'No,' Lukeson lied, furtively fingering Sally Speckle's letter in his coat pocket. It grieved him sorely when she had left without telling him. From the off, they had had a good and close working relationship; a relationship which had almost got very personal. He recalled that near kiss after the celebrations at the successful outcome of their first case,* when he had seen her home. And he could not help wondering what direction their relationship might have taken had that kiss materialized.

'If she'll get in touch with anyone in this den of inquity it'll be you, Andy.'

'Sally had . . . has a lot of friends in Loston nick, sir.'

'Popular officer, sure enough. But you know what I mean.'

'I'm not sure I do, sir.'

'Oh, come on, Andy. You and she were . . .' Doyle hunched

* See *Pick Up*.

his shoulders, obviously regretting he had begun. 'Well. . . .'

Miffed, Lukeson was not of a mind to let his superior off the hook. 'Well?' he challenged.

'Ah . . . close,' the CS mumbled.

'We were nothing more than working colleagues,' Andy Lukeson said. 'Very good working colleagues. But *only* working colleagues.'

'If you say so, Andy,' Doyle said uncomfortably.

'I do!'

Prodded by what he saw as Lukeson's stiff-arsed reaction, Doyle responded with equal gruffness: 'That wasn't the impression round here, I can tell you.'

'I don't give a tinker's what the impression was round here,' Lukeson exploded. 'That's how it was.'

'Keep your hair on,' Doyle cautioned. 'I have to admit that I thought what everyone else thought. But if you say that it wasn't so, then that's as it stands, man.' His sigh was gloomy. 'Hope this Watts business isn't going to turn nasty. We'll need to make quick progress on this one, Andy. Speckle put together a fine team, in which you played a very important part. I have every confidence that you and the team will come through with flying colours. Your success in nabbing Blake's killer will be fresh in mind, and will stand you and the force in good stead.'

Meaning that the press would, due to that success, give him and consequently Doyle, breathing space, Lukeson thought cynically.

'There's one more,' Doyle said. 'A fellow called Albert Dotty. Spotted hanging around a children's playground near Miranda Watts's school. Reported by a concerned parent to a community officer. Get to it then. Regular reports. Keep overtime to a minimum. In fact, think kindly of your pressured chief super and keep overtime out of the picture altogether. Good luck, Andy.'

'Thank you, sir. I'll do my best.'

'You always have,' Doyle complimented sincerely. 'That's why I'm handing this lot to you. Do Speckle and yourself proud.'

'I hope to.'

Lukeson had the door of Doyle's office open, ready to leave when: 'Oh, and DC Clive Bailey has been assigned to your team.'

He might be downright cynical, but Andy Lukeson reckoned that he knew the reason for Bailey's inclusion. Katherine Stockton's knight-in-shining-armour would also be media friendly. Doyle was living up to form. Any bad news, or news of a difficult nature, was always imparted when one was left with really no alternative but to leave. But this time, Andy Lukeson was bloody-minded enough to challenge his superior's decision; a decision that would, in his opinion, have more nuisance value than value added.

'Bailey, sir?' he queried tightly.

'Hearing becoming dodgy, is it Sergeant?' Doyle grunted, giving his attention to the papers on his desk.

The easy option would be to slip quietly away. But: 'Why Bailey?'

'Sounds like you don't like him.'

'It's not a matter of liking or disliking,' Lukeson said, instead of what had come first to mind, and that was that Clive Bailey was a prat. 'Bailey has been in the Training Division since he transferred here from Brigham. He'll be operationally rusty, sir.'

'Operationally rusty,' Doyle intoned. 'You sound like a telly copper. Clive Bailey, who admittedly can be a pain in the arse, has experience to bring to bear. He found Katherine Stockton, remember?'

'It's not likely that anyone will ever forget,' Lukeson said in exasperation.

'And so he should be proud of his achievement, Lukeson. If Bailey hadn't found Katherine Stockton when he did, Brigham might have had a body on their hands.'

'Then maybe we should ask DI Carter for his input?'

'Carter?'

'He headed up the Stockton team, sir. We might even ask Brigham to let us have him on loan.'

'Have you taken leave of your senses, laddie,' Doyle boomed. His reaction made it quite clear that he had not asked a question, but rather had reached a conclusion. 'Have a Brigham officer mucking about here in Loston business.'

'Well, sir, if DC Bailey has experience, wouldn't Carter fall into the same category?'

'Bailey is now a Loston officer, Lukeson.'

'I'm not sure I see the point, sir,' Lukeson said, a point which he understood perfectly. It was all a matter of nest-protection and no small amount of pride, both of which would, but should not, take precedence over bringing the guilty to book. Andy Lukeson had on many occasions attended meetings and courses where the *brass* had spoken robustly about cooperation and how *pulling together* was of vital importance. But in reality, most such sessions were the very definition of *hot air* which quickly evaporated at the end of the session. Good intentions were all fine, but protecting one's patch by far outweighed good intentions.

31

CS Frank Doyle struggled with what he was about to say, but finally settled for: 'Best to keep things in-house, Andy.' Then followed the stock reassurance: 'Of course, if at any point Carter can be helpful, I'll not hesitate to pick his brains.'

And the bloody moon will fall to earth, Lukeson thought.

'Look,' he said placatingly, Doyle was very good at placation when necessary. 'Knowing the ropes, having been through an abduction before, Bailey's help will be invaluable.'

He wasn't going to win.

'Just one thing before I go, sir. . . .'

'Yes,' Doyle asked cautiously.

'As I recall, Katherine Stockton never identified Samuel Curly as her abductor. In fact she never identified her abductor at all.'

'You sound like a one man band for Curly's innocence, Sergeant,' Doyle said frostily.

CS Frank Doyle's phone could not have rung at a more timely moment. Andy Lukeson left, headed straight to brief his team, still rankled by having DC Clive Bailey foisted on him without as much as a single word of consultation.

It was true that Bailey had found Katherine Stockton, but the commonly held view was that the child's rescue was due to a whacking great dollop of good fortune rather than any flash of brilliance on Bailey's part. He had even published a book (written more like a Hollywood thriller by a ghostwriter), much to the chagrin of his colleagues who had put in a hard slog, but had not had the luck which had favoured Bailey.

Thus, his freezing out in Brigham and his move to Loston.

There was nothing wrong with luck, except its fickle nature. Lukeson preferred competence and sound investigative procedure any day.

'Andy!'

'What now,' Lukeson mumbled. And, turning to Doyle by his open office door he added. 'Yes, sir?'

'Report of a female child's body. Thatcher's Lot.'

CHAPTER TWO

WPC Anne Fenning looked suitably contrite under Andy Lukeson's glare. However, reckoning that there was only so much contriteness to give, or that she should give, she said, 'I cocked up. But as I've said, I thought the woman was a dotty old dear. They're a penny a dozen. Lonely old dears who imagine all sorts of things. There was that woman last year who reported a murder in the flat above her, based on a man shouting that he'd kill her, and the screams of a woman. It turned out that the flat had been let to an actress who liked to rehearse, who had roped her boyfriend in to help her to, as she put it, achieve authenticity. That she did, sure enough. Besides, we're only human, and therefore we make mistakes.'

'I don't recall any criticism made,' Lukeson said.

'Not in as many words, no. But you had a face on you that would crack a mirror at a hundred paces! Oh shit! I'm sorry, Andy. First rule. Get a name, phone number and address. And have a trace put on the call.'

'Impressions.'

'Impressions?'

'Yes. You mentioned a woman who kept calling Hilly. The woman's keeper, carer, you reckon? As in nursing home, maybe?'

'I don't think so.' Fenning opined. 'If Hilly, presumably short for Hilda, was in a care facility, she'd hardly be left to wander around in a place like Thatcher's Lot, guv.'

'Good point. If she's elderly, but isn't a resident in a nursing home or some such place, she must live close by to the lot, I reckon. Mobile enough to get there, and lucid enough to report what she saw.'

'She did mention half an hour before as the time she witnessed the goings on in the Lot. So, assuming that she's getting on and not a strong walker, that would put her location pretty close to the Lot.'

'Good thinking, Anne,' Lukeson complimented. 'Any background noises that might get the search for her up and running?'

'Timber flooring. I heard the woman's footsteps as she approached, before Hilly hung up. Firm, purposful footsteps. Hilly was afraid of her. Hilly was not supposed to be on the phone.'

'An older domineering sister or relative,' Lukeson speculated. 'Fancy a cuppa?'

'Yeah. Lovely.'

'Off you go then, and bring one back for me.'

'You're a charmer, aren't you.' Fenning's cheeky retort brought a smile to Lukeson's lips. 'And there was me thinking that I was the Queen of Sheeba.'

'Nothing much we can do until the body, if there is in fact a body, is found. Unless the search team is very lucky, it could take a considerable time in a place like Thatcher's Lot. No hint as to where Hilly witnessed all of this?'

35

Fenning shook her head.

'Do you reckon that it's Miranda Watts who's been dumped, Andy?' Lukeson did not answer. But his glum expression spoke his thoughts. 'Back in a mo with the cuppa.'

'Throw in a sticky bun, eh.'

Andy Lukeson saw the name on the office door as Fenning left: DI SALLY SPECKLE. He immediately had a sense of intruding, even if it was only to keep her chair warm until she returned.

If she returned.

He had little time to waste, but he spent some time dealing with a degree of trepidation about how the team, Speckle's Team, would react to him taking over as their guv'nor. Annoyed by his self-doubt, anger took him over. 'You've got a kid to find,' he berated himself. 'And maybe her killer too. Get bloody on with it!' He spent the time until Anne Fenning returned familiarizing himself with Allen's progress to date, which wasn't much.

The phone rang, scattering Lukeson's thoughts.

'Found the poor mite, Andy,' Sergeant Harry Spencer, the team leader of the Thatcher's Lot search party informed him.

When Andy Lukeson and DC Charlie Johnson arrived in Thatcher's Lot, SOCO were already in situ, none too pleased, waiting for Alec Balson the police surgeon to arrive on scene – a displeasure which Jim Holmes (nicknamed Sherlock), the SOCO team leader, was not reticent about voicing.

'Where the hell is Balson?' he enquired brusquely of Lukeson, the second he put in an appearance.

'On his way, I expect,' Lukeson replied with equal brusqueness.

Holmes was a naturally aggressive sort, the kind of individual who got up Lukeson's nose. The SOCO leader was not a person with whom he got on, much too full of his own importance for Lukeson to have warmed to him. Holmes was a man who was forever strung out, or as close to being as did not matter. But the gathering of forensics being a tedious job, often in inhospitable surroundings and conditions, Lukeson could understand Holmes's impatience. However, Holmes not being one to hang about, in a job that needed an ability to deal with frustration, Lukeson couldn't help think that a change of job might be better for Holmes and everyone else.

'That's informative,' Holmes flung back. 'It's bloody ridiculous, isn't it. Police surgeons were fine in Hercule Poirot's heyday. . . .'

'Don't tell him Poirot was fictitious,' DC Charlie Johnson murmured in an aside to Lukeson. 'He might lose his marples.' He grinned impishly. 'Sorry. Couldn't resist that.'

'. . . But not now. The sooner they dump an old warhorse like Balson and replace him with a forensic pathologist the better.'

Talk of such had been doing the rounds for some time, but Lukeson hoped dearly that, as with many proposals which did the rounds, it would in time be shelved. Sid Fields, the present in-house forensic pathologist would be Balson's automatic replacement, and if the worst came to pass, Fields would be better than a complete outsider being drafted in. That was not to say that the powers that be would act logically. It was likely, based on past experience, that they would throw the baby out with the bathwater, particularly if it fitted in with their all-sacred budgetary requirements. Fields was a very competent man, but for scene-of-crime analysis, Balson – the lesser qualified but vastly more experienced of the two – possessed sharp instincts and canny insightfulness that made him a hard act to follow. Sid Fields was magnanimous enough to admit as much, having more than once been heard to say that he only confirmed what Alec Balson had already concluded.

Holmes continued with his gripe.

'I mean, it doesn't make sense in an age of technological and scientific wizardry to have a local GP doubling as a police surgeon. Maybe,' his tone became even more scathing, 'we could arrange to have murder committed outside of his surgery hours. That way we wouldn't all have to stand around having our *ghoulies* frosted in a stinking wood.'

Pushed too far, Lukeson exploded: 'Then why don't you find yourself a nice nine-to-fiver, and give us all a rest from your bitching!'

'Touchy,' Holmes sneered. Then, pouting his lower lip. 'Oh, dear. Missing Sally, are we?'

Seeing Lukeson's blood reach boiling point, DC Charlie Johnson stepped between his guv'nor and Holmes.

Holmes stalked off to join his colleagues who, *en masse*, cast a hostile glare Lukeson and Johnson's way.

'Thanks, Charlie,' Lukeson said.

'All part of the service, guv.'

The girl lay face-down. Lukeson gently turned her head to see her face, and was relieved to find that it was not Miranda Watts. His guilt was immediate. It was sad that any child should have died.

'Not Miranda Watts,' he informed Johnson.

'Never thought it was,' Johnson said. 'Just look at her gear.'

Idiot. How could he have been so unobservant. The girl was dressed in near rags, not at all the clothing of the offspring of such a wealthy woman as Sarah Watts. His compliment to Johnson was a back-handed one.

'You'll make a good detective one day, Charlie.'

The girl was pale, eyes bulging, hair unkempt and of poor quality. Malnourished. There was strain and no small degree of pain in her crimped, older-than-her-age features. Wizened, Lukeson reckoned, would fit the bill as a description. Her hard death had followed an equally hard life. Lukeson thought that it would probably have been better had she never been born.

Startled by Alec Balson's appearance from nearby bushes, Charlie Johnson leaped backwards, admonishing the police surgeon: 'You scared the shit out of me! How did you get here?'

Balson held aside the bushes from which he had appeared, to reveal a lichen covered path, his the only footsteps on it for a long time.

'Used to play cowboys and indians round here when I was a lad. I know every inch of Thatcher's Lot, dank mess that it is. Hello, Andy. Imelda Ledgrave,' he said mysteriously. 'Twenty odd years she's been dying from every complaint known to medical science. No convincing her that she's as healthy as a leaping flea. Probably live to be a hundred and twenty.' He donned the scene-of-crime outfit handed him. 'The missing girl?'

'No.'

'Better see what we have then,' Balson said, kneeling to begin his examination of the dead girl.

'Used to be pagan sacrifice offered here,' Johnson said, making conversation.

'There was a coven of witches hereabouts,' Balson said. 'Last reported on in 1938. A woman called Annie Blanc. Killed a young boy as a sacrifice to the Horned One, as she called Old Nick. Committed suicide to be with her Lord and Master, rather than face trial.'

Andy Lukeson cast a curious glance at the dead child.

'I'll check, Andy,' Balson said, second guessing Lukeson's thoughts about ritualistic killing.

'Can you hurry it up,' Holmes called to Balson. He pointed skywards. 'Rain on the way.'

Having had long experience of the crotchety SOCO, Alec Balson ignored him. 'Dead about ten hours give or take,' he told Lukeson. 'Badly treated and woefully neglected. Untouched, in a carnal sense. And she wasn't murdered.'

'Not murdered?' Lukeson was stunned.

'I think she probably died from an asthmatic attack, Andy. Likely brought on by fear or anxiety. See here.' Balson held up the girl's hands, emphasising her long uncared for nails with traces of dried blood under them. He then turned up the palms of her hands to show Lukeson the puncture marks of her nails where they had bitten into the flesh. He clenched his fist to graphically explain what he believed happened. 'There's older and newer blood,' he said. 'Indicating anxiety at different times which, I believe, eventually triggered the asthmatic attack that killed her. Or at least didn't help.

'It's my belief that this poor mite lived in constant and

persistent fear. Whoever subjected her to this torture needs to be caught quickly. And I hope when apprehended, the key will be thrown away. That's about it, Andy. Over to Sid Fields.'

'He'll only confirm what you've come up with, Alec.'

The police surgeon chuckled. 'That sounds like a compliment.'

'It is.'

'Won't be in the saddle for much longer, I'm afraid,' Balson said. 'The official thinking is that old war-horses like me have had our day.'

Holmes snorted.

'Have the powers that be said as much?' Lukeson asked, ignoring Holmes.

'Oh, yes. What was it the letter said ... "A review of procedures at the location of scene-of-crime have concluded that the services of a forensic pathologist might be deemed more appropriate in the future. A decision in this matter will in due course be conveyed to you." '

'Bastards!'

'Oh, time moves on, Andy,' Balson said philosophically. 'Change is all about us.'

'Much of it horseshit!'

'We must look to the future. A couple more years in practice, that's about it for me. Don't want to topple into the grave, stethescope dangling. Best be getting along. Prelim report ASAP.'

He looked down at the dead girl.

'Nail the bastard, Andy,' he said angrily. Having gone a few paces, Balson paused. 'Any sign of Speckle returning?' Lukeson shook his head. 'Pity. A damn fine copper, Sally Speckle. Cheerio, Andy.'

It might be the way he was hearing Balson's goodbye, but it seemed to Lukeson that it had a ring of finality to it, and he wondered if he'd be seeing Balson again in his official capacity as a police surgeon.

DC Charlie Johnson joined Lukeson, who told him about Balson's findings.

'Good.'

'Good?'

'If the kid had been murdered, it would be a complication we don't need.'

'A complication?' Lukeson said tersely. 'That's a little girl lying there. That's a whole lot more than a bloody complication! Someone caused her death, and dumped her like a sack of old potato peelings.' Johnson looked sheepish.

'I didn't mean the kid's death doesn't matter, Andy. I was only thinking that we have enough on our plate finding Miranda Watts.'

Knowing Charlie Johnson to be a caring and compassionate man and copper, Lukeson knew he had over-reacted.

'Sorry for bawling you out, Charlie.'

'I should have chosen my words better,' Johnson replied graciously.

Andy Lukeson said sombrely, 'A dead girl about the same age as Miranda Watts is, and Katherine Stockton was when she was abducted. Pattern you reckon?' he murmured thoughtfully. 'Where was she? What terrible ordeal has she been through, Charlie?'

'No ID?'

'No.'

'Why wasn't she reported missing, guv?'

'No one cared enough. It happens.'

Johnson looked down at the girl. 'Worlds apart. This Dickensian waif and the posh Miranda Watts. As I recall, Katherine Stockton was also from a well-heeled lot. What would this kid have in common with Watts and Stockton, Andy?'

'Gender and age,' Lukeson said.

'Was she sexually interfered with?'

'Balson says not.'

'Neither was Stockton,' Johnson said. 'A link? But it's been a long time since Stockton was abducted. Is it likely that a nutter could restrain himself for that long?'

It's been a long time since Samuel Curly was at large also, Lukeson thought.

'Maybe it isn't sexual at all,' Johnson pondered. 'Well, at least not in an active sense. In a kinky sort of way. Katherine Stockton was locked away in a caravan. It looks like this child was also locked away. . . .'

'Go on,' Lukeson urged his DC.

'Possession? A collector? Some twisted bastard who likes to watch or dwell on his victims die slowly.' Charlie Johnson's sigh was world weary. 'Ever wonder why we spend our time wallowing in the sewer of human existence?'

'Every day, Charlie,' Lukeson said sincerely. 'A check with Social Services will hopefully put a name to this little mite.'

Climbing up the slope leading up from the crime scene, Andy Lukeson looked back down into the gloom of Thatcher's Lot, where the girl's body was being prepared for removal, and felt as he had often felt in the weeks since Sally Speckle had opted out – lonely, disjointed and

dispirited. Had they become that close?
Or, rather, had *he* become that close?

CHAPTER THREE

Taking several deep breaths, Andy Lukeson strode resolutely along the hall to the designated incident room. Although resolved to take the briefing in his stride, the further along the hall he progressed, the more he realized that his newly acquired resolve was built on sand. It was never going to be easy to step into Sally Speckle's shoes because of the high esteem in which her colleagues held her, and also because, as a DS, he would have been seen as more team than leader. The only comparison he could draw with what he felt was that which had gripped him on his first day in school. A mixture of curiosity as to how he'd be received, and a numbing fear of the unknown.

Speckle would be a hard act to follow.

Coppers were slow to accept a new guv'nor, until he or she had proved their mettle, and that could take a long time. And, if found wanting, ranks quickly closed to make life impossible. Ground lost was never regained, and a career could be dead in the water in no time at all. If that happened, it soon became very obvious to one's superiors and a career adjustment quickly followed. This might, at best, mean a move sideways and at worst mean an early pension, suggested or sought.

But at least he was not taking over from Sally Speckle in a fuller meaning. Hopefully, remaining a detective sergeant would not create too great a gap between him and his colleagues.

Lukeson stepped into the incident room in what he hoped was a confident, jaunty manner. All heads turned his way, in a fashion he imagined they might if they were to peruse the occupants of an alien spaceship. The faces were the same, but what was going on in those heads? Each one would have their thoughts on who might be best to have taken over from Speckle and a nick being a close-knit community, there was no way of knowing who was for and who was against.

'Morning all,' he greeted.

'Morning all,' DC Helen Rochester mimicked. 'You sound like a village bobby from the fifties, guv.'

Rochester's cheeky impersonation brought a round of laughter which, though he chuckled along, Lukeson found disquieting. There was a balance to be struck quickly between being genial and being too genial – the classic guv'nor's dilemma. Too much geniality and discipline went out the window. Too much starch and goodwill was lost. There was, he'd learned, when he had stood in for Jack Porter, a very fine line between mentor and master, colleague and guv'nor.

Lukeson got straight down to business.

He put up a photograph of Miranda Watts on the white-board. Though everyone would be in the know, he would still treat the briefing as if Miranda Watts had just been reported missing, determined as he was, to make the investigation his own, and not be seen as rubber stamping

DI Allen's case.

'Miranda Watts. Nine years old. Abducted from Cherrytree Lane. Despite our best efforts, no sign of. Miranda Watts seems to have vanished off the face of the earth. As we stand, four possibles. Samuel Curly. Albert Dotty, Simon Bennett, who was Sarah Watts's live-in lover, and Watts herself.

'Sarah Watts?' WPC Anne Fenning questioned doubtfully.

'Unlikely, though possible,' Lukeson said. 'Can't be ruled out. Mothers have harmed their children before,' he reminded them, as he had Doyle. 'Top of the list,' Lukeson put up a file photograph of Curly. 'Out of lock-up less than a week. Inside for the abduction of Katherine Stockton over in Brigham seven years ago. Stockton was approximately the same age and social background as Miranda Watts. And . . .' Lukeson put up a photograph of Stockton beside the picture of Miranda Watts. 'Not unalike in appearance.'

'Almost a dead ringer,' DC Helen Rochester observed.

'A case of old habits die hard, eh,' said PC Brian Scuttle.

Lukeson looked beyond the main group to where DC Clive Bailey was seated. 'DC Bailey, Stockton's rescuer, has been assigned to help us.' Someone gave a little groan. 'And I'm sure that his expertise will prove invaluable.' A not-so-little groan. 'Case files have been made available by Brigham CID, so you will need to familiarize yourselves with their contents.

'Next up, Albert Dotty. No pic to hand. Likes to hang around children's playgrounds, does Albert. When questioned by the community officer, Dotty said that watching children playing raised his spirits. No previous.

47

'Moving on to Bennett. No pic. No form. Turfed out by Sarah Watts shortly before Miranda Watts went missing. Like Curly, Bennett, as of now, is nowhere to be found. Dotty can be found on the Clewbridge Estate.'

'The Clew,' PC Brian Scuttle snorted. 'Right sort of breeding ground for villainy.'

The Clew. Police jargon for a notorious Loston council estate.

'Not all residents of the Clew are a bad lot,' Lukeson said. 'There are decent people living in the Clew as well as the villain classes.'

Hearing his voice echoing back to him, Lukeson sounded terse, even pompous and prattish. He wondered if the assembled team was hearing him as he was hearing himself? Likely. There was a shifty unease which had not been there before. Had he struck the wrong balance already? A stuffed shirt. Full of his own importance.

Time to clear the air, he reckoned.

'OK, everyone.' Lukeson pulled up a chair, turned it wrong way round and straddled it cowboy style. 'Poacher turned gamekeeper is never easy for the new gamekeeper or his former poacher friends. But someone has to become gamekeeper, and for now, that's me. Some of you might agree. Others disagree. That's your right. As long as any opinions held or expressed do not interfere with finding Miranda Watts, that's fine by me. However, if those opinions become an issue, I'll not hesitate to act. Understood?'

DS Andy Lukeson's gaze swept the room.

'If anyone wants out, now is the time to leave. No hard feelings. In the long run, it'll be better all round.' A sombre silence settled over the room. 'I'll take that as a no, shall

I? Now, let me make one thing perfectly clear. I would much prefer to be present here as Sally Speckle's DS.'

After what seemed an age, thankfully, Scuttle broke the silence.

'Nine years old,' he exclaimed, casting his eye over the photograph of Miranda Watts. 'Could pass for thirteen or fourteen.'

WPC Anne Fenning agreed.

Scuttle continued: 'That's what gets these kids into all sorts of trouble. Parents who allow their kids to grow up before their time.'

'That's as may be,' Lukeson said. 'But we're not social workers or social commentators setting the world to rights. We're coppers. So let's leave our personal and private views outside the door.'

'She's a little Lolita, isn't she,' Scuttle persisted, as protective of his opinion as a pitbull of his bone. His persistence brought a scowl to Lukeson's face that would put a vampire to fright. 'OK, guv. Point taken.'

'Curly is probably the front runner,' Lukeson said. 'But don't settle for him, and find that he's not our man after all, while the real culprit flies the coop. A point of interest. Curly protested his innocence in court, and spent his entire time inside doing the same.'

'The prisons are full of innocent, hah hah, men, Andy,' Helen Rochester said.

'All I'm saying is not to close your minds and suffer coppers' blindness.'

'With the benefit of experience,' DC Clive Bailey said, all eyes on him. 'I reckon she hasn't gone far.'

Bailey was sitting a way off from the common herd – like an omnipotent being of wisdom might – which was no place for someone who was supposed to be part of a team to be seated. At best it conveyed an impression of not wanting to be there (which in Bailey's case was true – perfectly, content as he was to remain aloof from operational policing in the Training Division). At worst it imparted a feeling of superiority which could be petrol to flame.

Lukeson's reaction was awaited, and closely watched. He knew that what he did next would either make him the guv'nor. Or make him a spent force.

'Thanks for your opinion, DC Bailey,' he said smoothly, pointedly using the formal rather than the personal form of address. He placed the chair he'd been straddling firmly between Helen Rochester and Charlie Johnson. 'But I'd much prefer you'd join your colleagues to give your input, than sit in the corner like Little Jack Horner.'

The atmosphere crackled.

For a moment it was obvious that Bailey contemplated rebellion. However, recognizing that Lukeson was not for turning, he came and sat on the chair Lukeson had provided. Lukeson would have wished that the stand he had taken had not been necessary, but it had been a Hobson's choice. Lose the goodwill of one. Or lose the goodwill of all.

By now everyone would be aware that Clive Bailey had been assigned, not for his deductive brilliance but for his high profile, when the media would spot the similarities between Katherine Stockton's and Miranda Watts's abductions.

Grist for the PR mill, was Clive Bailey.

Like Sally Speckle, Lukeson hated the publicity and PR circus police work had become. Sometimes he feared that the need to avoid criticism might get in the way of sound and proper procedure. There had already been cock-ups which had let some seriously malicious villains back on the streets on some minor technicality due to the *results at any cost* mentality which had come to prevail. Nowadays, the smallest lapse in correctness was ruthlessly exploited by extremely expensive lawyers (often the kind who could only be afforded by cash-rich thugs) to the benefit of the wrongdoers and the detriment of their victims.

'In my experience,' Clive Bailey intoned grandiosely. 'There are three types. Planners. Watchers. Impulsives. The first will have a well thought out plan of action. Ransom will more than likely be the objective. This abductor will have cleared out quickly, probably before the police would even have become aware of the abduction. The second type takes pleasure from knowing that someone who thinks they're perfectly safe, is not. Watching is the real pleasure here. Like the proverbial predator, the Watcher closes in gradually on the prey. This abductor will have probably made himself known to his intended victim. Likes to get close, this one. Relishes the surprise of his victim when he pounces on them. The Watcher takes pleasure in shedding his sheep's clothing to reveal the wolf in hiding. And this one will also want to hang about to watch the plods chase their tails, will have an exaggerated opinion of his, or indeed, her own cleverness. And that sense of one-upmanship is often their undoing. A spider waiting to draw the fly into its web, that's the Watcher. He or she will have picked a bolthole close by. Usually mentally unstable, and therefore unpredictable. Lives in a fantasy world more often than not. Or simply evil personified.'

Had Lukeson tried, he would probably have been able to recall the exact page in Bailey's book about the Stockton abduction upon which he was drawing.

'And the third type,' Helen Rochester asked, seemingly intrigued.

'The Impulsive. Spur-of-the moment kind. No plan. Chaos when the enormity of what they've done – and the punishment in the offing, or disgrace and social exclusion if they're unmasked – will make them highly susceptible to act out of panic. The desire to cover their tracks becomes overwhelming. More often than not, in their rising panic, will want to rid themselves of what now becomes their problem. Motivation can be difficult to establish. There may not even be a motive. And if there is, it can range from the simplest to the most bizarre. When they work up enough courage to protect themselves from discovery they will act ruthlessly. Probably killing their victim in their by now insane desire to maintain their public standing and their fear of retribution.'

PC Brian Scuttle snorted cynically.

DC Clive Bailey's look his way was waspish.

'If you people don't want the benefit of my experience. . . .'

'Give your experience a rest, Bailey,' Scuttle snapped.

Lukeson stepped in, before all out hostilities broke out.

'Clive has given us an insight into types,' he said. Daggers of displeasure were sent his way, which he perfectly understood. No one liked a know-it-all. But he would not be deterred. 'Each officer here has a right and a duty to state it as he or she sees it. I won't have it any other way. Because somewhere along the way, what might seem inconsequential or positively daft, could be the key that will unlock this whole thing. So if you have something to say, say it, and no handbags.'

Scuttle took Lukeson up on his invitation, with a degree of forthrightness that Lukeson had not intended.

'You're talking rubbish, Bailey. Another book in mind, have you? What's it going to be this time. How I pointed the way to my fellow plods.'

'Leave it, Scuttle!' Lukeson commanded. But his hope, knowing Scuttle's no-holds-barred personality, was never on the cards.

'You're no flaming genius,' he told Bailey. 'Finding Katherine Stockton was no flash of brilliance. You got lucky, mate!'

Scuttle had stated the general opinion.

Lukeson sought some clever form of words to assuage Bailey's injured pride and Scuttle's bristling anger, but nothing came to mind. So he resorted to the well tried formula of master and servant. 'Shut it! Both of you!'

After a lengthy stand-off, Charlie Johnson said, 'Don't anyone strike a match or we're all gone up.' His witticism took the sting from the confrontation. Lukeson took the opportunity to put the briefing back on track.

'There's one other, perhaps not significant party, a woman called Sylvia Planter—'

'The medium?'

'Know her?' Lukeson enquired of Helen Rochester.

'Went out with this bloke once. Into all things supernatural. We went to one of Planter's seances.'

'What did you make of it all?' Lukeson asked.

'I didn't have an opinion either way. Still don't.'

'A load of old tosh, isn't it,' Charlie Johnson said. 'Give me a break.'

'Which leg?' Anne Fenning said.

'How droll,' Johnson shot back.

Rumour had it that Johnson and Fenning had spent an evening together of late, which had not worked out. The hostility of their exchanges, and their equally hostile demeanour towards each other now would seem to bear that out.

'Might I remind you of Adrian Brooks, Charlie,' Lukeson said.'*

'Where does Planter fit in anyway, guv?' Fenning asked.

'She recently attended a seance at the Wattses' house, during which she spoke of an *imminent* danger. The whole thing ended in a bit of argy-bargy between Sarah Watts and Planter about her fee. Then Miranda Watts went missing. Probably coincidence. But. . . .'

'Always a "but", isn't there,' Johnson grumbled, his nose a little out of joint.

'Now,' Lukeson put up a SOCO photograph of the dead girl found in Thatcher's Lot. 'We come to the dead girl found in Thatcher's Lot. No ID. Not reported missing. Due to her neglected state, I reckon that Social Services will be our best hope of putting a name to her. Of course she might not be from the Loston area at all. Significantly, about the same age as Miranda Watts and Katherine Stockton, but from a different world. Watts and Stockton come from silver spoon backgrounds. The child in Thatcher's Lot is a Dickensian waif. Not murdered. Died from natural causes. An asthmatic attack, Alec Balson

* See *Remains Found*.

reckons. Yet to be confirmed. But I've never known Alec Balson to call a cause of death wrong. He also thinks that the attack was probably brought on by fear. No ransom demanded for Stockton, or as yet for Watts. However, the child in Thatcher's Lot would not have figured for ransom.'

'A paedo ring?' DC Charlie Johnson wondered.

'It's a possibility which has to be considered,' Lukeson said.

'My money is still on Curly,' Scuttle said.

'I think that I should point out that Samuel Curly is a convicted kidnapper, not a convicted paedophile,' Clive Bailey said.

'Fiddly!' Scuttle grunted. 'The bastard just didn't have time to get round to her before you showed up.'

'Don't become fixated on Curly to the exclusion of all others,' Lukeson cautioned. 'Closed minds make for mistakes.'

'What if, for the sake of argument, Stockton's real abductor saw a chance to get up to his old tricks when Curly was released from prison. The police would have a real suspect in Curly. Might not look any further. It's not hard to imagine that Curly would be banged up again, letting Katherine Stockton's, Miranda Watt's and the kid in Thatcher's Lot's abductor walk away free as a bird, again. Just a thought,' Johnson added, when there seemed to be no one for or against.

'We have a witness who saw the dumping of the girl's body in Thatcher's Lot,' Lukeson said. 'Anne.'

Fenning brought the team up to speed on the phone call she had had.

'You didn't think to have it traced?' Johnson said critically.

Fenning shot Johnson a look that should have turned him to a pillar of salt.

Lukeson came to Fenning's rescue.

'Now this woman called Hilly seems to be elderly which, as Anne shrewdly pointed out, means that if she walks in Thatcher's Lot, she lives somewhere close to it. The door-to-door presently in progress in the area will hopefully unearth her. If not, possibly a GP in the area. Social Services, perhaps. Now tell me what you think.'

Lukeson played the recording of Sarah Watts's 999 call. When the recording finished, Helen Rochester observed:

'Not in bits is she. Not as upset as a mum whose daughter has gone missing should be.'

'Could have been buying a pound of butter,' was Anne Fenning's take on the recording.

'Keep in mind that, as CS Doyle pointed out, Sarah Watts is a tough-as-nails business woman,' Lukeson said. 'She'd be used to cold assessments and coming directly to the point. Which could make her sound like a bit of a cold fish.

'Anne. I want you here as an anchor and the keeper of bits and pieces. OK?'

'You're the boss,' she replied coolly.

Her dissatisfaction with her assigned role was obvious. He might have told her that as a team coordinator she was the best there was, but decided that had he to explain every decision he made there would not be much time for anything else.

For her part, Fenning felt like all behind-the-scenes workers who beaver away – unseen, unnoticed and uncredited when the time came for kudos. But as CS Frank 'Sermon' Doyle had so often preached, the police was not a democracy, so there would not be any point in protesting her role. She could only hope that in time, as in the wider workforce, the police also would be dragged kicking into the present.

Sensing Fenning's displeasure with her lot – which Clive Bailey would much prefer compared to mucking about talking to people he would not wish to pass the time of day with – Bailey said, 'If you'd prefer to be out and about, we could switch. You have to be good at organizing things in the Training Division.'

'As the guv'nor, I'll decide who does what and who goes where,' Lukeson said brusquely.

Expressions remained impassive. Those present might welcome his put down of Bailey. However it might also have been seen as him being guv'nor for the sake of being guv'nor. And Lukeson thought that, were he a team member instead of the team leader, his view might very well be of the latter than the former.

'Any questions?'

No one had.

'Then let's get out there and find Miranda Watts.'

CHAPTER FOUR

The country pile in which Sarah Watts lived was set, as one might expect of an Englishman's castle, in a sylvan haven of gently rolling countryside for hunting and shooting, lakes for fishing, and woods for whatever the gentry used to get up to in the woods. The house, previously the stately domain of a Lord of the Realm whose lineage extended back to Tudor times (a reward for giving the Papacy the boot when the Pope got up the nose of Henry VIII) had five years previously gone the way of many more companion properties. Lost to death duties and dwindling resources (the latter brought about by the last peer's largesse to too many fast women, too many large wagers on too many slow horses, unobliging roulette wheels, and ill-considered investments with stockbrokers whose advice had more insanity than sense) the family had been compelled to face reality and relinquish the house, ending their long and distinguished tenure. Over the years the family had produced several bishops, two generals, a whole basket full of colonels, three diplomats and an eminent cardiologist.

The obligatory wrought iron gates, attached to

limestone pillars adorned with a pair of languishing lions, swung open seconds after Johnson pressed the intercom button to announce: 'Police.' In a manner a village bobby might have in the days before everyone had rights, the big house ruled supreme and unchallenged, and the word litigation was, except in higher echelons, thought to be a surgical procedure, probably to do with birth control.

He drove through the gates which instantly swung shut behind them, giving a feeling of finality, as if getting back out was utterly at the discretion of some unseen master. 'Hope we don't run out of diesel before we reach the house,' Johnson said, looking up what seemed to be a never-ending avenue of trees, most of which were proud English Oaks with the odd interloper of indeterminate pedigree to break the monotony. 'All that strutting the catwalk paid off handsomely, eh. As I recall, didn't she come down with something a couple of years ago?'

'Tubercolosis. Ended her career as a model. Closed one door and opened another. When the TB passed, Sarah Watts proved to be a very shrewd business woman. And now one of considerable wealth.'

'The golden couple,' Johnson said. 'Danny Marlaux and Sarah Watts. Before Marlaux upped and left out of the blue.'

'I'm impressed by your degree of research, Charlie.'

'Research? No. Celeb mag gossip.'

'Celeb mag gossip?' Lukeson enquired wryly. 'You?'

'There was nothing else to read at the dentist's, other than a two year old copy of National Geographic,' Johnson said self-consciously. 'A big surprise, Marlaux moving out.'

'Surprised me also. Danny was, once he settled down, a bit of a homebird.'

59

'Danny?'

'I know Danny Marlaux from way back.'

'Didn't know that you moved in the champagne and caviar circle, Andy.'

'Danny Marlaux and I shared a desk at school. Used to always say that he'd end up in the racing game. Down at the bookies, everyone thought. Not as a trainer with swish stables, country tweeds and the obligatory Range Rover.

'Bowled everyone arse over when he and Sarah Watts, who was then a top model, became an item. Always the handsome charmer, was Danny. Women, young and not so young, were putty in his hands. His relationship with Sarah Watts finally opened the doors which he had always been pushing at.

'Got his first big break as a trainer from a consortium of footie managers. To everyone's astonishment, Marlaux, an unknown, turned a lead-legged nag into a winner. After that the sky was the limit. Sheikhs were lining up to get horses into the Marlaux stables.'

'Devil's Own. The name of the first Danny Marlaux winner,' Charlie Johnson said. 'My old man had a tenner on the nose. His mates down the Workingmen's Club thought he'd gone senile. But he had the last laugh. He's lived off the glory of that moment ever since. Seems to have been a marriage made in heaven, Andy. So why did the marriage go belly up?'

'Irreconcilable differences, the papers said.'

'Meaning Marlaux was playing away from home?'

'Don't reckon so. Like I said, Danny Marlaux sowed his wild oats. But when he settled down, that was that.'

'That was the Marlaux you knew, Andy. People change. Everyone does, don't they. If humans didn't change they'd be boring farts, wouldn't they. It's what they get up to that makes them interesting. Bloody Moses!' Charlie Johnson said in reaction to the wide sweep of gravelled forecourt the drive emerged onto. 'Loston United's ground would fit into a corner of this lot.'

The PC standing guard at the front of the house descended the steps in what Lukeson would call *reporter repellent mode* until, drawing closer and recognizing fellow coppers, he lost his fiercesome look and smiled benignly.

'Thought you were the press,' said PC Bob Long, running his tongue around his mouth as if to rid it of some foul taste. He cast searching eyes about. 'About all over the place, the blighters!'

'Not a sign of anyone when we arrived,' Johnson said.

'Oh, the buggers are much too clever to be seen,' Long said. 'Less than ten minutes ago I spotted one behind those bushes.' He pointed. 'With one of them cameras that can see up your ar— You know the kind of thing, sir.'

Bob Long had become suddenly conscious of Lukeson who, not long ago, he would have addressed as he had Charlie Johnson. When he had filled in for DI Jack Porter, Lukeson had been acutely aware of his former colleagues, with whom he'd have exchanged banter, calling him sir, much preferring the informality of his previous relationship with them. But he had come to realize that as a DI (even an acting DI) relationships had to change, and the camaraderie he had enjoyed so much had to be foregone because, giving orders, making demands and decisions – often difficult decisions – were functions which did not lend themselves to familiarity. In fact it had been the very master-and-servant nature of senior rank which had deterred him from taking the promotion on offer when Porter had called it a day.

'Lady Muck about, Bob?' Johnson asked.

'Yeah.' Long cast a glance over his shoulder to the house. 'Shall I. . . ?'

Lukeson nodded. Long hurried away. Less than a minute elapsed before he was back, beckoning them inside. 'Ms Watts is in the morning room, sir.' He escorted Lukeson and Johnson along a hall that appeared to be the length of an airport runway and the width of a motorway. Or perhaps that was some trick of the eerie light from the recessed wall lighting permeating the hall – the overall effect of which was to make the hall deeply depressing.

In fact the overall atmosphere inside and outside the house was depressing.

When Sarah Watts and Danny Marlaux had moved in, she had been at the height of her powers, commanding fantastic sums to appear at the world's top fashion shows, and even greater sums for product endorsements. Agencies queued round the block to get Sarah Watts's signature on a contract.

At the same time that Sarah's star was the brightest in the fashion firmament, Danny Marlaux's shone with equal, if not even greater, luminosity in the horsey heavens. His touch was golden. All the races that mattered were won by horses trained at the Marlaux stables, and Danny also had the knack of breeding nags that brought stud fees with many zeros through his letter box. Nothing could, it seemed, go wrong. But it was at that point that fickle fate turned against the golden couple. Sarah got TB, and Danny developed a fondness for cocaine, a very expensive habit which got ever more addictive and ever more expensive. The cocaine addled his brain and his business acumen to a disasterous degree and, like all addictions acquired to soften the blow of Camelot crashing down, the fool's powder took over completely, until Danny Marlaux's day was spent coming down from one high and going to the next in his efforts to shut out reality. Deals were cancelled. Get-out clauses activated, and so-called friends, who had been ever-present in good times drifted away, finding excuses to be somewhere else, anywhere else, rather than in the Marlauxs' company, fearful of being mentioned in the now not-so-glossy mags to which Sarah Watts and Danny Marlaux had been cruelly relegated.

Sarah Watts had handled her decline much better, showing a surprising resilience and clawing her way back to the top. She had sucessfully launched a string of cheap jewellery shops which provided lots of glitter and gloss to please those who could not afford the real thing. Her selling line was: 'Looks like a million. Costs a pittance.' Those in the so-called know had rubbished her business plan, but two years later, with shops franchized and opening somewhere almost weekly, those who had cast scorn on her were now firmly hiding in the bushes. The venture had, when it seemed that she too would have to face reality and relinquish the house, secured her country pile.

However as Sarah Watts achieved spectacularly, Danny Marlaux failed miserably. The Marlaux magic had deserted him in his personal and horsey life. Now the best the Marlaux stables could produce were horses which made up the numbers at meetings far removed from the glamour of previous victories.

PC Bob Long knocked on the door he had stopped outside, with the reverence of a Buck House lackey. Lukeson had expected a regal 'Enter,' but instead, got a narky: 'Oh, do come in!' When Long opened the door to let Lukeson and Johnson pass inside, a young woman sporting close-cropped dark hair, her face suffused with anger, brushed Lukeson aside as she stormed out of the room, an apology not even considered. Long announced: 'Detective Sergeant Lukeson and Detective Constable Johnson, ma'am.'

Lukeson waited for the expected blast of trumpets which, had they sounded, would not have surprised him.

'Don't forget to curtsy, me lad,' Johnson said, obviously his socialist side aggrieved by Long's display of cap doffing.

Bristling, Long marched back along the hall. Lukeson and Johnson entered the morning room.

PC Brian Scuttle gave a little shiver when DC Helen Rochester turned into the narrow country lane leading to Sylvia Planter's cottage. 'Creepy,' was his verdict. The road was bordered on both sides by huge gnarled brooding trees, the skeletal branches of which had reached across the road to intertwine with the branches of the trees opposite, like crones shaking hands – the effect was a dark, depressing tunnel. Funnelled, the fresh breeze which was blowing became an eerie banshee, more common to the Yorkshire Moors of the Baskerville Hound than Loston's pleasant agricultural countryside.

'How could anyone live down this lane?' he asked. 'Looks like a horror movie set.'

The Planter cottage matched the approach to it,

crouching like some evil entity, covered in heavy dark ivy which had encroached onto the roof, as if determined to smother the cottage and those within. Its small leaded windows reflected the intermittent daylight through trees stirred by the breeze, giving (at least to Scuttle's mind) the impression of evil eyes watching. The garden showed an odd glimpse of its former glory, long since lost in the rampant untamed undergrowth. For Brian Scuttle, it resembled a long-neglected country churchyard, and he had always avoided cemeteries like the plague. He had an intense aversion to all things to do with death and decay. When they got out of the car, the smell of rotting vegetation was pungent to the point of gagging.

'I've smelled sweeter tips,' he grumbled.

'It's November,' Rochester said. 'The countryside is not at its best.'

Looking around him, Scuttle said, 'This place hasn't been at its best for a long time. Not hard to imagine evil here, is it.'

'Aura, Brian. All-important in Planter's line of work. It would be easy to believe that spirits are part and parcel of this place.'

'Work?' Scuttle scoffed. 'Tomfoolery, designed to fleece the gullible.'

Rochester went forward and knocked on the cottage door with the heavy brass knocker in the form of a wriggling snake. 'Be ready to duck the vampire bats when she opens up,' she teased Scuttle. True to the setting, when it opened, slowly, of course, the door had the obligatory creaking hinges. The woman who answered, Rochester thought, was perfect casting. Thin. Ethereal. Huge dark eyes that, once engaged, were difficult to disengage from. The clothes she wore, like her persona, was pure wardrobe Romany gypsy. However, the expensive shoes she wore gave the lie to her impoverished image. A man appeared in the hall behind her and hovered, seeming uncertain as to what he should do, Rochester reckoned he was ready to do whatever was required of him. 'Sylvia Planter?'

The woman seated in the bay window at the far end of the room looking out on gardens that would give Kew a run for its money, though recognizable, was no longer the pin-up who gave men, young and old, a rush of blood. Sarah Watts's startling beauty had been replaced by a steely resolve which had hardened her features and made her eyes; eyes which turned on Lukeson and Johnson, cold and unwelcoming. How cruel illness and time, a relatively brief time, can be, Lukeson thought. Not so long ago, Sarah Watts had the ability to bring on male breathlessness. Hers was now a face that would have one casting one's mind back, searching for a name to go with a sense of vague familiarity.

Sarah Watts studied Lukeson curiously, obviously trying to place where she might have seen him before. He was not of a mind to enlighten her. She quickly lost interest, probably having decided that he was a face in a crowd, one of the multitude of faces she would have seen over the years in her high-profile career, obviously of no great importance. Had she concentrated a little longer, she might have placed him as Danny Marlaux's guest at a garden party some years previously.

'Which is Lukeson, and which is Johnson?' she asked. Lukeson clarified for her.

Sarah Watts switched her gaze from Lukeson to Johnson; going from one of inquiry to one of disdain. Feeling the vibes of Charlie Johnson's resentment, Lukeson questioned his wisdom in having him along, knowing Johnson's sometimes abrasive nature when confronted by those he considered parasites – meaning anyone with more money than the average post office savings account. Lukeson knew from previous experience of the garden party about Sarah Watts's equally confrontational personality, shown in a brief but tempetuous argument with Danny Marlaux in his presence.

'Sergeant?' she questioned, not bothering to hide her disgruntlement.

'DI Allen has had an unfortunate accident, Ms Watts,' Lukeson explained. 'I'm—'

'A detective sergeant,' she interjected. 'Frankly, I would have thought that Allen's replacement would be of a more senior rank.' Lukeson refused to be drawn. 'Well, I suppose I shall, as a mere taxpayer, have to be satisfied.' She pointed to a regency chair, the partner of the chair on which she was seated. Lukeson sat. There was no such invitation extended to Charlie Johnson. 'Well?' she enquired brusquely.

'Just a few more questions,' Lukeson said.

'Would it not be preferable to be out securing my daughter's return, instead of *just a few more questions*? What more questions can there be that I haven't already answered for Inspector Allen? Did he not take note of my answers?'

Andy Lukeson had not liked Sarah Watts the first time he had met her at the garden party with Danny Marlaux, and nothing had changed.

'I've fully informed myself of DI Allen's enquiries, Ms Watts.'

'Then why waste time, Sergeant, going over old ground?'

Lukeson was struggling to keep his cool, but he'd be damned if he'd let it show. Charlie Johnson had no such inhibitions. His stance and glare were definitively that of a bulldog.

'This is a follow up interview, Ms Watts. First interviews after a crime are understandably fraught and emotional, and something might have been missed or ommitted through no one's fault.'

Sarah Watts held Lukeson's gaze unflinchingly.

'I'm never fraught. And even less emotional, Sergeant Lukeson.'

DC Charlie Johnson's face said: Ain't that a fact!

'And I never omit anything.'

She turned and snatched up a newspaper on a table behind her. She turned it towards Lukeson to show him a photograph of Samuel Curly, looking suitably villainous. It would not have surprised Lukeson to learn that the image had been creatively enhanced, a pictorial statement to match circulation boosting reportage. She did not need to explain the purpose of showing him the newspaper. He had read the newspaper article which was highly critical of the police having lost sight of Curly. 'You let the bastard get away,' she said accusingly. 'This man, this horrible creature, a convicted sex offender, just out of prison for abducting a child, and now within days of his release Miranda's gone missing. How bloody careless can you people get!'

'Samuel Curly is not a convicted sex offender,' Lukeson said.

'Oh do spare me, Sergeant,' Watts snorted. 'He wasn't a sex offender because he hadn't the time to offend.'

It was a commonly held view.

'It was several days before the young girl was found,' Lukeson pointed out.

'Are you defending this monster?'

'No, ma'am. What I am trying to explain is that the police can only act on the decision of the courts. Curly is not a registered sex offender, and therefore once he had his sentence served he did not require supervision. But when we locate Curly, which I'm confident we shall—'

'Confident we shall,' Watts scoffed. 'Curly was under your noses and he vanished. I'll not hold my breath that you'll find him again.'

To try and reason with Watts would be flogging a dead horse, so Lukeson accepted her derision which, in all fairness, was understandable.

'Did Miranda normally make her own way home from school, Ms Watts?' he queried.

'She preferred to.'

'Did she always get what she preferred?'

Sarah Watts fixed Charlie Johnson with an icy stare. 'Do I detect a note of criticism, Constable?'

'Just asking a question, Ms Watts.'

'It's a tough world. The younger you learn to cope, the more likely you are to succeed.'

'I would have thought that with your high business profile and obvious wealth, leaving her to walk home unescorted was risky to say the least.'

'In today's world, getting out of bed in the morning is risky,' Watts snapped. 'Too much security is counterproductive. Focuses attention.'

'And too little is, as has been shown, foolish and dangerous,' Johnson said uncompromisingly.

Andy Lukeson thought Watts's philosophy a hard one. His personal view was that children nowadays, as compared to when he had been a lad, often had their childhood stolen from them by over-ambitious parents.

'I could have had her picked up in a chauffeur driven limousine, Constable, but that would only have set her apart. Miranda would have hated that. And, of course, it would isolate her from any friends she might make. She wasn't good at making friends, so I didn't want her to lose the ones she had.'

'Miranda was of a quiet personality then?' Lukeson asked.

'She withdrew into herself a little when my husband and I broke up.'

'Had Miranda been seeing someone?'

'Someone?' Watts said tetchily. 'You mean a psychiatrist? She was quiet, Sergeant. Not disturbed.'

Was?

Andy Lukeson noted the use of the past tense, but came to no decision as to what it might mean.

'Lonely, perhaps?'

'All children, and adults too, feel lonely sometimes. It's the human condition.'

'Lonely people often do things to bring attention to themselves, Ms Watts. A cry for help.'

'What exactly are you implying, Sergeant? That Miranda's gone off on her own to focus attention on herself? Your so-called cry for help?'

'Your marriage break-up can't have been easy for her.'

'Many marriages break up.'

'And as a result there are many victims, Ms Watts. With Mr Marlaux not here, and you being away a lot, the emotional upheaval she must have been experiencing could not have been easy to cope with.'

'You make me sound like a frightful parent. Let me set you to rights, Sergeant. Busy woman, I most certainly am. But never too busy to not be aware of what was happening in my daughter's life. Miranda liked to be independent. She would not wish to be molly-coddled. And I agreed with that. The fact is that these are changed times. At nine years of age, you and I would have been children, but nowadays the gap between childhood and young adulthood is so brief that it's barely quantifiable. Youngsters now want to rush out of childhood.'

Sarah Watts looked wistfully into the garden.

'Life's so full one day, and the next it's so terribly empty.'

'Did Miranda always make her way home alone?' Charlie Johnson questioned.

'Mostly.'

'Along the same route?'

'I suppose.'

'You suppose? But you can't be sure.'

'Children are creatures of impulse, Constable. Not fitting into a routine is attractive and a touch rebellious to them. Cast your mind back. How often were you told to do so-and-so, just for the hell of it did the opposite, and found the experience and the deceit exciting. It was your secret. Knowledge no one else except you had.'

Charlie Johnson recognized the scenario which Sarah Watts had sketched.

'So we can't assume that she had a known routine, then?'

'I think that's what I just said.'

'Were you not concerned that, being the daughter of a high-profile—'

'Of course I was worried,' Watts snapped. 'But as I've explained, Miranda liked—'

'To be independent,' Johnson interjected tersely.

'And as I've also said—'

'You encouraged her to be so.'

Watts and Johnson glared at each other. Lukeson stepped in.

'Was Miranda ever picked up from school, Ms Watts? On rainy days, that kind of thing.'

'On the odd occasion, Simon would pick her up.'

'That would be Mr Bennett?'

'Twenty nine years old. Cambridge educated. Worked in the City for a while. Didn't like it very much, work, I mean. Likes cricket. Plays when he can be bothered, but rarely bothers. An overall shit, but rather accomplished between the sheets.'

Her laughter was short and mirthless.

'Shocked, Sergeant?' She did not wait for Lukeson to answer. 'I'm thirty seven years old. Pretty much a has-been in the looks department. And I spend eighteen hours a day, most days, running a business. Men like Simon Bennett come packaged. Know their place, and their duties. It's easier and much more convenient and hassle-free for a woman like me to hire in.'

'How long have you and Mr Bennett been lovers?' Lukeson asked.

'Oh, about a year, give or take.' She scoffed. 'Lovers implies moonlight and romance, Sergeant. My relationship with Simon was nothing as delicate as that. I needed, he provided, would more accurately describe our arrangement. Simon Bennett was a very dutiful purveyor of pleasure. And I, in turn, was a very generous benefactor.'

'You're a very honest woman, Ms Watts,' Lukeson said.'

'And now you're thinking, heartless cow. While she's humping the hired help, she let's her child fend for herself, and then gives you a whole load of old codswallop about independence.'

Lukeson remained impassive. Charlie Johnson tried, but was not remotely successful.

'Was Bennett and your daughter . . . *chummy?*' Johnson asked.

'Chummy? You mean was he attracted to her?' Johnson raised a quizzical eyebrow. 'No!' Anger flashed in Sarah Watts eyes. 'Do you think I'd have kept him around if they had been, as you say, *chummy.*'

Charlie Johnson was not in a placatory mood, and of a mind to point out that she had not kept Bennett around.

'By your own admission, you were away a great deal.'

'Mrs Clark was here, Constable,' Watts stated.

'That would be the housekeeper?' Lukeson queried.

'Yes.'

'Always?' Johnson pressed.

'Yes. Well. . . .'

'Go on, Ms Watts,' Lukeson prompted.

'Mrs Clark's sister is very ill. She lives alone. In the last couple of months she's had to go to her at short notice. If I could, I always got someone in. . . .'

'But it wasn't always possible,' Johnson said. 'Leaving Bennett here alone with Miranda?'

'I'm not sure I like what you're suggesting, Constable,'

Watts said. However, though her response was frosty, there was no doubting the worry which Johnson's line of questioning had given rise to in her. 'Are you suggesting that Simon Bennett abducted Miranda?' she enquired quietly of Lukeson. 'Or perhaps that she went voluntarily with him?'

'We have to consider that Bennett might have filled a gap in her life when Mr Marlaux left,' Lukeson said. 'Why did you finish your relationship with Mr Bennett?'

'Nothing sinister, I can assure you. Simon had shown me all his tricks, and I had tired of them. It's as simple as that.'

'Cut up, was he?' Johnson asked. 'Having his, ah . . . *services* dispensed with.'

Andy Lukeson wished that Charlie Johnson would clear off and grind his axe somewhere else.

'We had what I would describe as a frank but civilized exchange of views, Constable. Cambridge educated, Simon was not into the more robust exchanges that can often accompany R&E.'

'R&E?'

'Nothing kinky, Constable. Rejection and ejection.'

'And you? Are you into robust exchanges, Ms Watts?'

'Oh, yes. I'm a cat and dog person. Had I not been, I could not have survived in the fashion and business worlds. You're barking up the wrong tree. Simon Bennett hasn't done a mischief.'

'That's very positive, Ms Watts,' Lukeson said.

'That's because I believe what I say, Sergeant.'

'You don't think it coincidental that your daughter went missing a short time after your bust up with Bennett, then?'

Sarah Watts looked at Johnson witheringly.

'Bust up is not how I would describe Simon's leaving.'

Johnson snorted. 'Bust up too downmarket, eh?'

Lukeson grimaced. There were times when he wished Charlie Johnson might be more diplomatic and less confrontational. But Charlie was Charlie. He was a good copper, if somewhat abrasive.

'Did Mr Bennett leave handsomely rewarded for his . . . tenure?' Lukeson enquired. He had thought that tenure would sound better than asking bluntly if she had paid him off, but it did not. Then again, there was no delicate way to make the enquiry he'd just made.

Sarah Watts laughed, surprising Johnson as well as Lukeson. Both had expected a tirade. 'Let's say that he was adequately rewarded for his,' her grin was impish, 'input.'

In for a penny, in for a pound, Lukeson thought.

'Can you define adequate, Ms Watts.'

'Ten thousand pounds.'

'Very generous. Terms and conditions?'

'That once he'd gone, he'd never come back.'

'Didn't fancy a reunion then?' Johnson snorted.

'I never allow the past to revisit me,' Watts said. 'I like to, in true British fashion, forge ahead, you might say.'

CHAPTER FIVE

Sylvia Planter's wary look was one which Rochester and Scuttle knew well. Planter had had dealings with the law before.

'DC Rochester and PC Scuttle. We've come about a seance you held recently at the residence of a Ms Sarah Watts.'

'With her kid gone missing, snotty cow, I thought you lot might be calling round,' Sylvia Planter said. 'I did warn her, but she wouldn't listen.'

'May we come in?' Rochester asked.

'Can I stop you?' Sylvia Planter stepped aside to let them enter a decidedly depressing house, all bottle greens and dark browns. All part and parcel, Rochester thought. Plunge depressed people further into depression and they become more susceptible, suggestible, and reliant. All part of the con.

Planter's inclination of her head in her protector's direction was barely perceptible, but the message, probably passed a million times before, was readily understood. He vanished into a room further along the hall. Helen Rochester noted that the room door did not click shut, which probably meant that he was listening.

'Will this take long?'

'I don't expect that it will,' Rochester said, when she might have said: 'It will take as long as is bloody necessary.'

'I don't want you in the way,' Planter said, as they passed inside. 'I've got someone coming. A woman whose husband passed on recently. She knows he made a will, but it's gone missing. We're hopeful that my spirit contact will be able to shed some light on its whereabouts.'

'I see,' Rochester said, neutrally.

'I doubt very much if you do,' Planter responded sharply, closing the cottage door to plunge the house into even greater darkness in the absence of the natural light coming through the open front door. 'You have, at the very most, ten minutes.'

As PC Brian Scuttle went past, Sylvia Planter placed a gentle hand on his arm. 'She's at peace, Constable.' Scuttle shot Planter a startled, nervous look. 'All her suffering is over, and she's very happy.'

Helen Rochester noted Brian Scuttle's sudden pallor. Sylvia Planter led the way along the hall.

'What was all that about?' Rochester enquired of her partner.

'A good friend of mine, an old girlfriend in fact, died a hard death a couple of days ago.'

Helen Rochester now understood Scuttle's pallor.

'A shot in the dark, Brian.'

'Some shot,' he said.

'Come on then,' Planter said plaintively. 'Do hurry.'

She had paused outside a room at the end of the hall, directly across from the room into which the man had gone. Helen Rochester supposed that it was her imagination in full flight, but her unease about going further into the dark and depressing house was very distinct. Scuttle, also, showed a degree of edginess that was not the norm for him.

'I keep minimum lighting,' Planter said, by way of explanation for the funeral gloom. What she said next did nothing to calm Rochester or Scuttle. 'The spirits, who are constantly around us, prefer shadow to light.' Her pause, hopefully only to heighten the sense of drama, was not reassuring. 'Especially the darker spirits.'

'The darker spirits?' PC Brian Scuttle enquired in a voice not much above a whisper, as if he were fearful of disturbing some malign entity close by.

'Yes. The spirits who visit from a place where no light ever reaches.'

'Hot there, is it?'

Planter ignored his feeble attempt at levity. She opened the room door and entered. A dingy yellow light seeped out of the room.

'The things a copper has to do, and the places he has to go,' Scuttle mumbled.

'No need to hurry away,' Sylvia Planter said. 'My visitors won't be staying.'

'Who's she talking to?' Scuttle enquired of Rochester. 'She's taking the piss, right?'

'Come along then,' Sylvia Planter said, a touch annoyed. Scuttle stood just inside the room door, his gaze sweeping the room. 'No need to be afraid of the dead, officer,' she said. 'You're never alone with the dead.'

'I'd prefer flesh and blood company, if you don't mind,' Scuttle said.

'Please. Sit.'

Rochester sat, but when Scuttle went to sit in a comfy armchair, Planter said, 'Not there. Peter is already occupying that seat. Knew Richard the Lionheart very well, did Peter.' Brian Scuttle backed away from the armchair. 'The chair behind is free.'

'I'll stand,' Scuttle said.

'Would you like Arthur to bring some refreshments?' Sylvia Planter asked. 'Tea? Coffee? Perhaps something with a little more bite?'

'Nothing, thank you,' Rochester said.

'Does that rule still apply in these liberal times. The one about not drinking on duty?'

'Yes, it does.'

'Makes sense I suppose.' Sylvia Planter's laughter was surprisingly bubbly. It made one want to laugh along. 'The last thing we'd need is a whole crowd of pissed coppers.'

'About this seance you held at the Watts house. . . .'

'Oh, that,' Planter said off-handedly, pulling on the single, curling, coarse black hair in the cleft of her chin which Rochester had earlier noticed and had been repulsed by. In fact it had been the first thing she had noticed about Planter. The hair was a revolting blemish on an otherwise perfectly proportioned face. She was pale but the pallor suited Sylvia Planter. In fact her drawn appearance served to give her, considering her line of work, a sense of the hereafter. Considering Planter's overall appearance and demeanour, it would not be difficult to believe that she might indeed have contact with the spirit world. 'Ms Watts,' she said the name with utter disdain, 'having had second thoughts about having held the seance, threatened to report me to the police as a charlatan. She didn't, did she, report me to the police?'

'Not that I'm aware of,' Helen Rochester said.

'These people. They invite you along, and when they hear something not in keeping with what they would like to hear, they get into a right old lather.'

'During the seance, you made a reference to an *imminent danger*. Can you be more specific?'

'If Watts hadn't gone off like a bloody cannon, I might have been able to be more specific. But because that silly woman ended the seance and did not allow me to explore further with my spirit contact, Miranda Watts has been abducted. If I had been allowed to go on, I'm sure Inspector Armitage would have enlightened us.'

'Inspector Armitage?' Scuttle questioned.

'My spirit contact. A police inspector. In fact, although he was not the officer in charge of the hunt for Jack the Ripper, he took a keen interest in him and was about to reveal the identity of Jack when, on his way to check the last piece of evidence which would have confirmed the Ripper's identity, he was run down by a carriage which did not stop. There was never anything done about the accident. The reason being, he says, was that it was not an accident, but murder, to stop him revealing the lofty personage who was responsible for the gruesome murders of those young women.

'What would their lives matter compared to the unmasking of a bigwig. No doubt that kind of thing is going on right now, too.'

Brian Scuttle exchanged a *bloody hell* look with Helen Rochester.

'What exactly did you tell Ms Watts?' Rochester asked.

'That her daughter was in imminent danger,' Planter

said impatiently.

'From what, or whom?'

'That's the point, that silly woman broke the circle and ended the seance.'

'That's all you told Ms Watts then? That Miranda Watts was in imminent danger?'

'Yes.'

'Was she not curious as to what this danger might be?'

'Oh, she was too much the carping bitch to think about that. Do you know, the more I've thought about it, I think she got into a rant to avoid paying me.'

'How much did she not pay you?' Scuttle asked.

'Five hundred pounds.'

'A tidy sum.'

'Well in keeping with my talents,' Sylvia Planter said haughtily.

'But not an excessive sum for a woman of Sarah Watts's considerable wealth,' Helen Rochester said.

'The rich become rich because they watch the pennies, dearie.'

'A bit alarming, don't you think. Telling someone that a loved one is in danger and leaving it at that?'

Sylvia Planter snorted derisively. 'Loved one. I wouldn't have thought so.'

'Oh, why do you say that?' Rochester queried.

'Mention of her daughter to Sarah Watts had waves of negativity flooding over me, the kind of negativity associated with great anger and frustration.' She considered long and hard before stating: 'I would suggest that rather than Sarah Watts loving her daughter, she would rather. . . .'

'She would rather?' Rochester prompted, when Planter

seemed of a mind not to continue.

'Be rid of her,' she said finally.

'Rid of her?' Scuttle questioned.

'Look, all I can say is that I sensed these negative feelings. But I can't possibly give a definitive reason for them.

'Can't Inspector Armitage help?' Scuttle scoffed.

Sylvia Planter was disdainful rather than miffed. She made a point of addressing Helen Rochester, while ignoring Scuttle. 'It's not uncommon for a busy parent such as Sarah Watts, empire builder that she is, to find a child more an obstacle than a gift. I'm sure that, as police officers, you encounter this kind of situation reasonably often when neglect is present. There was a darkness enclosing Miranda Watts. A very dark and a very evil event was predicted. Unfortunately, at that point there was still time to act. But. . . .'

Sylvia Planter shrugged.

Excepting the odd ruffle of feathers, DS Andy Lukeson wondered about Sarah Watts's calm. He might have expected weeping, recrimination, anguish, anger. He would not have expected practicality and pragmatism. After all, her nine year old daughter had gone missing, at a time that *missing*, more often than not, was a precursor to *murdered*.

'I've just thought . . .' Sarah Watts had Lukeson's and Johnson's absolute attention. 'He liked Cornwall.'

'Bennett, you mean?' Johnson checked.

'Yes.'

'Any particular part?' Lukeson asked.

'He mentioned St Ives a time or two. Cornwall was

Simon's bolt-hole when things got on top of him and he needed to get away.'

'From?'

'Oh, nothing in particular,' she said vaguely.

'Got depressed, did he?'

'Don't we all, Sergeant.'

'How depressed would depressed be?'

Sarah Watts shrugged.

'Morbidly depressed, perhaps?' Lukeson asked.

'He'd go inside himself. Become withdrawn.'

'On medication, was he?'

'He wasn't a nutter!'

'Who was his doctor?'

'I don't know. He'd go to London every now and then. He had worked in London. So I suppose his doctor was there.'

'A pharmacist, then,' Lukeson said.

'Not around here. I assumed that with his doctor being in London, his pharmacist was too.'

'Did you ever see this medication?' Johnson asked.

'No. I didn't want Miranda exposed to someone popping pills. So I made it a strict rule that Simon should take his medication out of view of her.'

'Were you not concerned?' Johnson queried.

'Concerned? No. Is there anyone nowadays who doesn't pop pills for one reason or another.' She asked quietly and unexpectedly, 'Do you think Miranda is dead, Sergeant Lukeson?'

Sarah Watts being a woman who would not suffer being fobbed off, Lukeson saw no point in evasion.

'There is that possibility, Ms Watts,' he said.

'Rid of her?' Rochester said, regarding Sylvia Planter's

remarks about Sarah Watts's feelings, or lack of them, towards her daughter.

'It's an honest opinion,' the medium said. 'It's what I felt then and now.'

'Vibes, eh?' Scuttle intoned sceptically.

'You think I'm quite batty, don't you,' Planter challenged Scuttle. Mad as the proverbial hatter, Scuttle's expression said. 'You'd think that I was talking utter rot, if I told you that right now there's a woman dressed in what I'd describe as colonial dress standing alongside of you. But there is.'

Scuttle spun round and knocked against a cheap self-assembly bookcase from which a framed photograph crashed to the floor. The back of the frame popped off and the photograph of a young girl fell out. Conscious of his clumsiness, he picked up the photograph and laid it on top of the bookcase along with the shattered frame.

'Don't worry,' Planter said. 'No harm done. Don't even know why I keep a photograph of Miss-High-and-Mighty around. My daughter,' she elaborated in response to Rochester's visual query. 'Not my flesh and blood. Adopted. Too grand to be a Planter,' she snorted. 'Gone back to her own name of Tompkins.'

She sighed reflectively.

'The whole thing was a terrible mistake. I should have known that she could never have replaced Sadie.' Planter became pensive. Rochester waited. 'A silly, stupid accident that need never have happened. All my fault, too. We were on a weekend break at the seaside. Laurence – Sadie's dad – and me. Dead against the idea, was Laurence. I should have listened. But we had had a bit of a dust up, like any husband and wife might, and I was getting back at him.

Dead against, was Laurence,' she repeated. 'Sadie walking along the prom wall.'

Pain filled Sylvia Planter's face at the memory of that weekend.

'Despite Laurence's misgivings, I gave in.' Her smile was sadly reflective. 'Sadie could wind me round her little finger. She took a tumble and fell on to the beach. She didn't fall far, but it was far enough for her to break her neck.

'I couldn't have another. Sadie was a one-off. Fortunate to have had her. Laurence thought that adopting would lift me out of depression. Eventually, I gave in and got Linda.'

She shook her head woefully.

'It never really worked out. To be honest, Sadie's ghost never left. Linda came loaded down with self-pity and angst and added to my grief. Well, there really never was a chance that we could bond. I hardly ever see her now. And I think that suits us both.'

Sylvia Planter laughed mirthlessly.

'Thinks she's Lady Muck because she works for Letty Hosford over at Brate Hall as a dogsbody. She'd have you believe that she runs the place. But she's about as important as last week's potato peelings.' She snorted contemptuously. 'Fancies herself as a writer, no less. Imagine. Little Linda Tompkins a writer. Whatever next.'

Sylvia Planter's gaze settled on the wall clock.

'Good grief! You must go now. My visitor will be arriving any minute.' She shushed Rochester and Scuttle out of the room, as if they were pets who had behaved badly.

Before leaving, Rochester asked, 'Do you really think that Sarah Watts might have harmed her daughter?'

Sylvia Planter did not answer the question specifically.

'It's not as uncommon as you might think. Some mothers don't bond with their child and, of course, the other way round also. Sarah Watts was at the top of her profession as a model when she became pregnant with Miranda. I recall reading in a magazine at the time her saying that being pregnant could have been better timed.'

Now that she had mentioned it, Helen Rochester remembered reading the same magazine article and had thought that Sarah Watts had sounded very bitter and resentful.

'Like many women,' Planter went on, 'after pregnancy she never quite got back the appeal she had before. Pregnancy steals away some women's vitality, don't you think? And, after all, stretch marks on the belly is not the stuff of catwalk queens. Overnight, Sarah Watts had gone from exotic temptress to being just one of a herd of ageing females. From tantalizingly sexual, to merely adequate. Don't you think that it's possible that she might have grown to hate the cause of this. I know that I might,' she admitted honestly.

'She's made a remarkable career, post modelling,' Rochester said, feeling obliged to restore Sarah Watts somewhat.

'Driven, that's Sarah Watts,' Planter said unsympathetically. 'Driven people can be obsessive. And, of course, there was the break-up of her marriage to Danny Marlaux. Some men go right off their wives after pregnancy. Makes them feel trapped, I suppose, when a woman goes from girlfriend to mum.'

'You don't like Sarah Watts very much, do you?'

Sylvia Planter turned to Brian Scuttle.

'A bit full of her own importance, if you ask me. A trait which she passed on to her daughter, I might add.'

'You know Miranda Watts?' Rochester asked.

'I wonder . . .' Lukeson said. 'Jealousy. Revenge. . . . 'Strong emotions.'

'Evil if they're allowed to fester,' Sarah Watts said. 'Have you spoken to Georgina Adams, Sergeant?'

'Georgina Adams?'

'One of Miranda's teachers. Nervy. Uptight sort.'

'Should we have?'

'Perhaps,' Watts said thoughtfully. 'There was some . . . no, considerable angst, between her and Miranda.'

'Why was that?'

'My fault, I'm afraid. The Cross factor.'

'Sounds like the title of a sixties spy novel,' Charlie Johnson observed.

'Robert Cross, that would be. Adams and he were colleagues. The handsome hero type. We met at a school function.' Sarah Watts shrugged philosophically. 'At the time, Simon Bennett was becoming tiresome. Cross was amusing. Let's just say that he showed potential. But it all fizzled out a couple of weeks later on a weekend trip to Brittany. It was raining. It was dreary. The hotel was substandard. One might say commensurate with a teacher's salary.'

Charlie Johnson thought that bitchy came easy to Sarah Watts.

'And dear Robert proved about as exciting as a damp squib on Guy Fawkes. The packaging proved to be much more attractive than the goods. You know the kind of thing. One wonders what one saw, blah blah blah.'

Andy Lukeson thought that when Sarah Watts put in the knife, she had no qualms about twisting the blade. He had never liked her very much, but now his dislike of her was unequivocal. However, despicable as her personality might be, he admired her honesty.

By her study of Lukeson and Johnson, it was obvious to both men that she had little difficulty in reading their thoughts. It did not trouble or deter her one jot.

'Robert Cross and Georgina Adams had had a brief fling which Adams hoped to reassurect, God knows why. After the abysmal failure of our liaison, Cross took himself off to Leeds, I believe. Adams had to blame one of us, and she chose me.'

'How long ago was this?' Lukeson enquired.

'Can't be precise. Six months, thereabouts. It was not something one might store away for one's old-age golden moments collection. Adams came to the house on a right old rant after Cross took flight. Went on about how she'd even the score with me, that kind of thing.'

'A woman scorned, eh,' Johnson said. 'Dangerous species.'

'Vindictive enough to abduct Miranda to get back at you, Ms Watts?' Lukeson wondered.

Sarah Watts thought carefully before replying. When she did, she'd lost none of her venom. 'Georgina Adams hasn't much going for her, Sergeant. She must have thought all her Christmases had come at once when Robert Cross took pity on her, his words not mine. I suppose, deprived of his attention, she might react badly. I'd be too tough a nut to crack, so doing a mischief to Miranda could be her way of settling old scores with me.'

'Did you report this incident to the police?'

'No. If I reported to the police every time someone threatened me, I doubt if you'd have the manpower to cope.'

On the evidence so far, both Lukeson and Johnson could believe that.

'A lot of enemies, then?' Johnson asked.

'You don't really live life on your own terms without making enemies, Constable.'

Not recalling anything in Allen's reports about Georgina Adams, Lukeson checked: 'Did you tell DI Allen about Adams, Ms Watts?'

'No.'

'Why not?'

'Somehow it didn't seem important until now.' It seemed extraordinary to Lukeson that she should not have made Allen aware of Adams and her possible involvement. But he also knew that shock played tricks with one's mind and perception. 'Miranda should never have gone to that piddling little school in the first place. She wasn't the type to fit in. To fall in line, in a one size fits all establishment.'

'Non-comformist, was she?'

Watts shot Johnson a waspish look. One thing was for sure, if Sarah Watts had been Eve and Charlie Johnson had been Adam, temptation would never have come to pass.

'She had a mind of her own, which I encouraged her to have,' Sarah Watts said defiantly. 'I had planned on a private school. But my husband of the time thought that there was merit in a state education.' She snorted. 'And when it seemed that Miranda might be coming round to an acceptance of my way, her father would pop round. He'd remind me, in Miranda's presence, about my conspicuously humble beginnings, pointing out that I had not done too shabbily without the benefits of a posh school, and sink the idea.

'Thing is, Danny Marlaux never quite shook off his humble beginnings. Liked to think of himself as a socialist.' She scoffed bitterly. 'Of course that, like all committed socialists, never stopped him from enjoying a capitalist lifestyle. He always made a point of telling everyone about his lowly beginnings, whereas I saw no merit at all in revelation.'

From his pocket, Lukeson took a photograph of the girl found in Thatcher's Lot and handed it to Watts.

'Have you ever seen this girl?'

Sarah Watts sat bolt upright. 'This girl is dead.'

'Afraid so.'

'About Miranda's age. Had she been missing too?'

'Not reported missing. She's something of a mystery at the moment. You're sure you've never seen her?'

'No. Found, you say. Where?'

'A place called Thatcher's Lot.'

'Thatcher's Lot. Poor mite.'

'Know it, do you, Thatcher's Lot?'

'No.'

Lukeson wondered if she was lying. It seemed to him that the way in which she had said Thatcher's Lot had echoed the desolation of the Lot itself. And 'poor mite' seemed to say that Thatcher's Lot was the worst of all places to be found. He was undecided as to whether he should press her on the matter, or leave it be for the time being. He chose to file it away, to be retrieved if required. Meanwhile, he'd ask Johnson if he had heard Sarah Watts as he had.

'Murdered?'

'No. Natural causes.'

'I don't understand. If she died of natural causes, why was she found in Thatcher's Lot?'

'There can only be one reason,' Lukeson said. 'Reporting her death in the normal way wasn't possible. Which means that her death, though from natural causes, still involved a criminal act.'

'Can I be frank, Ms Watts,' Charlie Johnson said.

'Have you been anything but frank, Constable?'

'I believe that your knowledge of Thatcher's Lot is a great deal more than you'd have us believe. Why would you. . . ?' Lukeson held his breath while Johnson paused to chose his words – *word*, as it turned out, no punches pulled. 'Lie.'

Good old Charlie. Never one to pussyfoot about when a hammerblow could be delivered. Lukeson had the question he had intended to ask but it was only answered after a pain-filled half-minute.

'I was only a short time in Loston when I went for a walk in Thatcher's Lot. I had much to ponder on. It seemed to be a place where the peace I was looking for could be found. I was wrong. Very wrong indeed. While walking there I was attacked. The man tried to rape me. But fortunately I was able to fight him off.'

'Did you report *this* to the police?' Sarah Watts shook her head. 'Why not?'

'I'd gone through a year when every newspaper and magazine I picked up had *poor Sarah* articles. Before and after kind of articles. Sarah Watts catwalk queen. Sarah Watts TB patient. Two sides of the coin stuff. Healthy and vibrant. Gaunt and spent. The last thing I needed was

Sarah Watts attempted rape victim.

'I was finished with my past and working hard on my future. A media circus I could do without. Contrary to the old adage that all publicity is good publicity, it is not. Particularly when you're trying to raise the kind of capital I needed.'

'Did you see this man?' Lukeson asked.

'No. He was hooded. Does it matter now? It was a long time ago and best forgotten.'

It might matter a great deal, Lukeson thought. If the man who had tried to rape Sarah Watts, and been frustrated, had returned to even the score by abducting her daughter. A check on rapists and would-be rapists who had recently been released from prison was now a matter of urgency. Starting with those who liked to hide their faces from their victims.

Looking at the photograph of the girl found in Thatcher's Lot, Sarah Watts suddenly exclaimed: 'Oh, God!' She sprang to her feet and began pacing.

'There is nothing to link this girl to Miranda,' Lukeson said.

'How can you be sure? You don't know anything about her. How she got to Thatcher's Lot. Who put her there. To say that there's no link to Miranda is pure speculation,' she finished crossly. 'How could she have gone missing, and her disappearance not been reported to the police?'

Lukeson changed track.

'You held a seance recently. . . .'

'Has that bloody Planter woman complained? I threw her out of the house quite justifiably. Bloody charlatan! She was hired as an entertainment for some guests, and she ratted on about this *imminent danger*, as she termed it, which her spirit contact – a Victorian police inspector no less – had warned her about. Who believes that rubbish? So what was intended to be a bit of a lark turned into a creepy load of old tosh about a dark evil presence around Miranda! So, as I say, I gave her a hundred pounds, four hundred short of what she was demanding, and threw her out.'

'Old tosh?' Johnson said. 'Your daughter has gone missing, Ms Watts. Where did you find this medium?'

'On a park bench.'

'On a park bench?'

'I was walking in the park, felt a bit tired and sat down. Someone had left an astrology magazine behind. I flicked through it, saw Planter's advertisement, and got the now rather silly notion, in hindsight, that she might add a bit of spice to what would be a dreary evening with dreary guests. I've always had an interest in spiritualism.'

'This Planter woman must have been very upset.'

'Furious.'

'Did she threaten any retaliation?'

'Not really.'

'Can you be more specific?'

'Oh, a lot of hot air about upsetting her friends in the spirit world. That they were dangerous entities to upset. She used the word vengeful to describe them.' She held Lukeson's gaze. 'Spirits can't bodily abduct someone, can they. But. . . .'

She switched her look from Lukeson to Johnson and back again. Ridiculed and turfed out, Planter might, was obviously the group thought.

'Did Miranda and Bennett hit it off?'

'Hit it off, Sergeant?'

'I believe you know what I'm asking, Ms Watts,' Lukeson said firmly.

Understanding Sarah Watts's anger, Andy Lukeson remained silent and patient. 'He'd bring her little gifts out of the blue. Tell her she was pretty, that kind of thing. All harmless.'

'Was Miranda upset when he left?'

'Yes.'

'How upset? On a scale of one to ten.'

'Ten,' she said quietly.

'My understanding is that Simon Bennett came into your daughter's life at what was for her a very vulnerable time, when you and Mr Marlaux parted company. Perhaps in her vulnerability Miranda became closer to Bennett than she might othewise have.'

'A surrogate father, you mean?' she snorted dismissively.

'And when Bennett left. . . .'

'It's daft, Sergeant.'

'What is?'

'What you're suggesting.'

'And what am I suggesting, Ms Watts?'

'That Miranda has gone off with Simon, of course!'

The silence held for a long time, before Lukeson said, 'We'd like to see Mr Bennett's room now.'

'Inspector Allen had it gone over with a fine tooth comb.'

'Still. If you'll lead the way, Ms Watts. We'll also need the names of the other participants in the seance.'

'Is that necessary? They're valuable business clients.'

'They'll have formed impressions and opinions which we'd like to have. And anyone else who may have borne a grudge. Perhaps while DC Johnson and I are looking over

Mr Bennett's room, you will draw up a list.'

Sarah Watts led the way out of the room.

'Did you meet Miranda when you were at the Watts house?' Rochester asked Planter, resisting her attempt to shoo her off the doorstep. Since she and Scuttle had gone inside, what seemed an age ago, but in fact was less than fifteen minutes, it had begun to rain, adding to the dreariness of the setting.

'No. Not at the Watts house. As well as being a medium, I am also a grannie.' It was difficult for Helen Rochester to imagine Sylvia Planter as a grandmother. She simply did not fit the role, or at least what she thought a grannie should be. 'Darren, my estranged daughter's son attends dance classes.' Her tone of voice conveyed what she thought of such, in her opinion, an unmanly activity. 'Wants to be a ballet dancer. A strange boy, my grandson. Miranda Watts attends the same classes. They're about the same age, so they became quite friendly. Darren is always on about her. I think he fancies her, if nine year olds can fancy. In more harmonious times, I collected Darren from the dance studio a couple of times. I met Miranda Watts then.'

'Was that why Ms Watts availed of your services?'

'She didn't even know I'd met Miranda. She phoned me up, having got my number from an advert I ran in an astrology magazine.'

'And you didn't mention that you knew Miranda?'

'No. I didn't think she'd appreciate the hired help knowing her daughter.'

'When last did you see Miranda Watts?' PC Brian Scuttle enquired.

95

'About two months ago. And I was here with Arthur recovering from the flu when Miranda Watts was abducted.'

'I didn't ask you where you were.'

'Just anticipating your next question, Constable. Shall I have Arthur verify what I've just told you?' she enquired of Helen Rochester.

'That won't be necessary.'

Rochester suspected that, even if Planter's alibi had not been rehearsed (had it needed to be), her mind would be quick-witted enough not to be caught off guard.

'Linda fools herself that one day Darren and Miranda will. . . .' She laughed cruelly, the bronchial nature of her laughter evidence of the respiratory damage inflicted by her heavy nicotine habit. 'Silly bitch! Dear, oh dear. That would never do. Lady Muck's little treasure hitched to plain old Darren Tompkins.

'Besides, I suspect that when Darren's hormones sort themselves out, his interest in Miranda Watts or any other female will disappear.'

'Might we have your daughter's address?' Rochester enquired of Planter.

'Whatever for?'

'If your grandson and Miranda Watts were friends, Miranda might have been round at her place. Miranda just might have mentioned something.'

'That's a shot in the dark.'

'Yes, it is,' Rochester conceded. 'But you'd be surprised how many shots in the dark hit a bullseye.'

'She'll not welcome you,' Planter warned.

'Not copper friendly, your Linda?' PC Brian Scuttle queried.

'Is anyone?' Planter replied scathingly.

'I promise to be at my most charming.'

'Like an alligator spotting a tasty meal, eh,' Planter scoffed. 'Mason Court. Flat . . . sorry. Apartment 41,' she finished plummily.

'Mason Court?' Scuttle checked.

'A bit posh for my Linda, you're thinking.'

'I'm sure PC Scuttle intended no offence,' Rochester apologized, furious with her heavy-handed colleague.

'He's right,' the medium said matter-of-factly. 'Linda's got a *friend* who pays the rent.' Her mood became malign. 'Let's say, in these politically correct times, he's not English.

'Where from?' Scuttle asked.

'London. Born and bred.'

'You said he wasn't English just now.'

'I meant, not real English,' Sylvia Planter said. The cottage gate creaked. 'Oh, gawd. Mrs Lacey!'

Rochester and Scuttle looked behind them at the woman whose eyes were fixed with suspicious curiosity on the uniformed Scuttle.

Raising her voice, DC Helen Rochester said, 'Nice to meet a law-abiding citizen, Madam. Nowadays, not many dog owners believe in having a valid licence.'

Lacey, on hearing this came forward and politely inclined her head to Rochester and Scuttle. Sylvia Planter ushered the woman inside, and quickly closed the door.

'Quick thinking, that,' Scuttle said. 'Not that I'd have bothered.'

'What do you make of all of that?' Helen Rochester enquired, leading the way along the treacherous moss-covered path.

'Barking!' was Scuttle's forcefully expressed opinion. He rolled his eyes. 'A copper who almost nabbed Jack the Ripper. Pull the other one!'

'It was an experience, wasn't it,' Helen Rochester said thoughtfully.

'You don't believe that batty old bird, do you?' Scuttle asked in stark disbelief.

Rochester hunched her shoulders. 'I don't know what I mean. Or what to think.'

'Tell you what,' Scuttle said, getting into the car. 'When we get back to the nick, we'll all join hands and form a circle round the guv'nor's desk, and ask Inspector Armitage the name of Miranda Watts abductor.'

'You're such a bloody cynic, Brian,' Rochester grumbled.

'I much prefer realist.'

'You don't have any specific belief, do you?'

'No.'

'Then how can you have such a closed mind. If you don't believe in anything, then you should be open to everything.'

'The Planters of this world are in it to squeeze hard cash out of very vulnerable people, Helen. People who are ready to clutch at any straw. But I do have another thought, if you'd like to hear it?'

'Go on then.'

'Miranda Watts was in danger, because Planter and her minder were that danger. Eh?'

'If they were that danger, Brian. Why would they signpost it?'

'Misdirection? Point a finger, and while everyone is looking in that direction, you can quietly go about your business in the opposite direction. What's the one thing a kidnapper needs most, Helen?'

'You're the deductive genius, Brian. You tell me.'

'Time. Time to cover their tracks.'

'Sylvia Planter hasn't gone very far.'

'You don't get it, do you.'

'Obviously not.'

'Sometimes, the best hiding place of the lot is right on your victim's doorstep.'

Helen Rochester studied Scuttle.

'Are you saying that Sylvia Planter might have Miranda Watts secreted away in her cottage, Brian?'

'Or nearby. While everyone else is watching air and ferry ports. All the while assuming that distance is some far off place.'

'Oh, come on. Would she have invited me to search the cottage if she had Miranda Watts there?'

'A gamble. The chances were that you wouldn't. And by offering, she would have allayed any suspicions you might have had. Maybe we should go back and search now.'

'And if we find nothing?'

'We'll be in the shit.'

'Right. And her motive for doing this? That we know of, no ransom demand has been made.'

'What if ransom is not the reason for the abduction, Helen. What if Miranda Watts has been abducted for a more sinister reason than mere ransom?'

'You know, the one aspect of police work I detest most of all, is the *what if* bit.'

PC Brian Scuttle chuckled. 'That's most of it, then.'

Helen Rochester punched out a number on her mobile. 'Anne. Run Sylvia Planter through the computer, see what you come up with.' Getting into the car, she enquired of

Scuttle: 'What was all that about someone being at peace, Brian?'

'Oh, it's nothing.'

'If it's nothing, it surely knocked you back.'

'Like I said, an old girlfriend of mine died a hard death last week. But if you think for one second that I believe that Planter has a line to the next world. . . .' He snorted derisively. 'These people spew out that kind of rubbish. There's always someone around who's had someone who's died, or whatever.'

'So you don't think there's anything in all this medium stuff?'

'Nothing at all,' Scuttle declared.

DC Helen Rochester let it go. But even now, it was plain that Brian Scuttle had had the wind taken out of his sails.

CHAPTER SIX

DC Clive Bailey was reluctant to get out of the car when PC Robert Chapps parked in front of Block 3 on the Clewbridge Estate, known to the police simply as the Clew. 'Block 3,' Chapps informed Bailey unnecessarily, seeing that BLOCK 3 was emblazoned over the entrance.

'What a depressing bloody kip!'

Chapps looked round him at the overflowing garbage, empty beer cans, cars that were half-cannibalized or totally burned out, and the constantly moving debris blown about by a fitful breeze. 'Yeah. Not exactly the Hollywood Hills, is it.'

'Why do people stay here?' Bailey wondered.

'Nowhere else to go.' Chapps eyed Bailey. 'Don't like this end of the job very much, do you?'

'No,' Bailey stated honestly, and then, pompously: 'My skill is in training.'

'To each his own,' Chapps said, his interest in Clive Bailey's distress fleeting. Getting out of the car, he told a group of sullen teenagers, their detestation of the enemy as they saw it, intense, 'Don't touch. Got it?'

No one answered. He had not expected that they would. He waited for Bailey to get out of the car, if he ever would. When he eventually did, his nostrils twitched.

'What's that stench?' he enquired of Chapps.

'The drains are bunged up again. Never worked right to begin with. But I suppose that's all right if you're poor.'

'Lazy,' Bailey grunted, and berated the assembled teenagers. 'Haven't you lot got anything better to do?'

'Ease off on the spurs,' Chapps advised.

'You're talking to a superior,' Bailey snapped.

'We're on our own,' said Chapps stiffly. 'We don't want a full blown riot, now do we? We'd probably end up as hamburgers before back up arrived.'

Though irritated by what he perceived as Chapps's insolence, Clive Bailey had enough reasoning left to see the wisdom of the PC's cautionary advice.

'We're wasting valuable time standing around here,' he said brusquely.

'The Clew is what it is because no one gives a toss,' Chapps said. 'The council bung them in as tight as rats in a coffin ship's hold and walk away. A case of out of sight, out of mind.'

'Spare me the socialist claptrap,' Bailey responded hotly. 'Haven't this lot ever heard of self-help?'

Right wing ideology (indeed sometimes extreme right wing ideology) was not uncommon in police forces which, Chapps thought, might account for the continuous and persistent alienation of the police from the less fortunate and downtrodden. He also knew from experience that argument contrary to Bailey's view was in the main unwelcome, and depending on who heard it, could be career ending. Being well into his thirties and still a PC was probably down to the kind of stance he had taken just now.

'Are we going to stand around all day being intimidated,' Bailey grunted.

Chapps went ahead to clear a path through the teenagers crowding the entrance to block 3. Well attuned to yobbo behaviour, the standard insult of pig and filth were old hat and ignored.

'Dotty been 'anging round the kiddies playground again, has he?' asked a hard-faced teenage girl, already world weary.

'Dirty old git!' said another, equally hard-faced, her demeanour suggesting that even at her young age she had given up on life, expecting nothing from the future other than what she had already known in her short life.

'I seen him, sittin' in his clapped out motor near the playground,' said the first girl who had spoken. 'Rummagin' under his overcoat.'

Much to the amusement of her friends, she gave a very graphic physical elaboration of what she thought Albert Dotty's actions had been.

'Lovely style, Julie,' a youngster sneered. 'Might fancy a bit o' that meself.'

'Oh, piss off, Benny. You ain't worth the trouble!'

'Slag!'

'Watch it!' said another youth threateningly.

'She givin' to you now, Alfie,' Benny taunted. 'You're at the end of a long line. I'd watch it, in case I caught somethin' nasty.'

PC Robert Chapps stepped in niftily, when Alfie lunged towards his tormentor. 'Settle down,' he barked.

'I'll do you,' Alfie threatened Benny.

103

'Shut it!' Chapps commanded.

'He insulted my bird,' Alfie ranted.

'Any trouble, and I'll know where to come calling,' Chapps said.

The young girl whose remarks had caused the disturbance, sniggered. 'Ain't you a sad sack, Alfie Clark. A quick feel round back of the flats don't give you no rights over me.'

'A quick feel,' Benny mocked. 'What was all that stuff 'bout you crawlin' 'way exhausted then, Alfie?'

'You never, Alfie Clark,' said the girl. She slapped the unfortunate Alfie across the face with every smidgen of force she could muster.

'I never said nothin',' the chastized Alfie whined.

The unfortunate Alfie became the butt of the laughter which followed.

Chapps had to work hard to prevent trouble of a serious kind breaking out. 'Go four different ways,' he ordered, when the group began to move off.

The girl became the peacemaker.

'Let's forget this whole thing righ'? And you'd be more useful pullin' Dotty in for that kid who's gone missin',' she told Chapps and Bailey.

'You seem pretty certain that we should,' Bailey said.

'That's 'cause I seen the old bastard hangin' 'bout outside her school an' all.'

'When was this?'

'Whatcha' doin', Julie,' said another youngster in the group. 'You don't help no coppers.'

'Dotty's a dirty old git, ain't he. How would you like it if it was your sister he took a fancy to, eh? And don't tell me what I can or can't do, righ'!' Defiantly, she told Bailey, 'A

104

coupla days before she went missin'. There was Dotty, sittin' in his clapped out van, lookin' kinda . . . kinda. . . .' She searched about for an appropriate description from her limited vocabulary of Dotty's demeanour, and settled for: 'Kinda dreamy, know wha' I mean? Watchin' them kids come outa school.'

Katherine Stockton had been bundled into the back of a van by her abducter. DC Clive Bailey wondered how long Albert Dotty had had his van.

'Yonks,' was the girl's response to Bailey's question about the duration of Dotty's ownership of the van. 'I was just a nipper.'

'Did you report this to the police?' Bailey queried.

'Report it to the pol. . . ! Don't be daft. No one round here reports nothin' to the filth! Come on, you lot!' She walked away. 'The air round 'ere is beginnin' to smell, you reckon.'

'That's plod bum gas, I reckon,' said a pale, lanky, hollow-eyed youngster, scratching his arm.

Chapps thought that if he pulled up the sleeve of the youngster's tatty hoodie, he'd find needle tracks. 'Leave them be,' he advised Clive Bailey when he seemed of a mind to become official. 'Don't push. You've got more than any other plod ever got on the Clew.'

The door of flat 26 had not seen paint for a very long time; had it done, it would be completely at odds with the general decrepitude all round. Chapps was poised to knock when a woman yanked open the door. 'Thought they was goin' to have ya,' she said, referring no doubt to the gathering at the entrance to the flats. 'Little tykes, the lot of 'em.' Her glance went from Chapps to the plain-clothes

Bailey. 'Brung the brass, I see.'

'Mrs Dotty, is it?' Bailey enquired.

'Yeah.' She sneered. 'Is that an arrestable offence then?'

'We'd like to talk to your old man,' Chapps said, before the suffusion in Clive Bailey's face manifested itself physically.

'Wha' 'bout?'

'Get him and we'll tell him,' Chapps said sternly.

For a moment, Liz Dotty's prematurely aged face set in stone, but then, knowing from long experience that in the end cooperation with a police request was inevitable, her bulldog expression softened. 'Better come in then, hadn't ya,' she said grudgingly. 'Don't want nosey-parker biddies gettin' no earful of me business, do I.' Leading the way along the grotty hall to a room at its end, she called out: 'Filth, Albert. He's been expectin',' she confided to Chapps, and enquired: 'Who's the tailor's dummy, then?'

'DC Bailey. I'm PC Chapps. And you mind your mouth,' he cautioned her.

'Looks like your DC Bailey is goin' to shit hisself. Not that the stench would make any diffrence 'round here. Oh, and you'd better watch for Yoyo.' On cue, a snarling pitbull came from a room just ahead. 'Have your ghoulies off for fun, would Yoyo.' She laughed mockingly. 'Particularly partial to plod attachments, ain't ya darlin'.' She picked the pitbull up in her arms. The room was a bathroom. 'Likes to kip in the bath, does Yoyo. Now you be good,' she chastized the pitbull. 'Don't want no trouble with the queen's plods, now do we.'

'Wha'cha warn 'em for, Liz,' rebuked the beer-bellied man who came from the room to which Liz Dotty was leading them, attired only in none-too-clean underpants.

106

Liz Dotty laughed. 'I call 'im ever-ready Al. Know wha'
I mean?' She rubbed Dotty's bare belly as she passed
inside the room.

'Save on dog food, wouldn't it, if Yoyo had their guts for
grub.'

'Naw, that would be real cruel, sweetface,' Liz Dotty
sniggered. 'We wouldn't want Yoyo to eat poisoned meat,
now would we.'

Going ahead, Dotty draped himself across a filthy
couch, stretched, and broke wind.

'I told ya not to have that Chinese,' Liz Dotty
complained. 'Chinese gives him terrible wind. Never did
have efficient bowels, did ya lover.'

Liz Dotty sat on the couch beside Dotty, legs spread,
showing a total disregard for modesty. Clive Bailey
thought that the Dottys were a well-matched pair from
the lower end of the human chain.

'DC Bailey has some questions, he'd like to ask,' Chapps
said, hoping that Bailey's pallor was not the precursor to
a fainting spell. Should he pass out, they'd be laughed off
the Clew. Say something, man, Chapps thought, when
Bailey looked sheepishly at him.

'Think the cat's got his tongue, Liz,' Dotty said. 'This
goin' to take long. Down the pub last night, so I had Liz
record Corrie for me. I was just 'bout to run the DVD when
you lot turned up.'

'It will take as long as it takes,' Bailey barked, sparking
suddenly to life, much to everyone's surprise. He crossed
to the television and switched it off.

Good for you, Chapps thought.

'Oooh!' Liz Dotty hugged herself. 'Forceful sort. Makes
me come over all giddy.' She cuddled up to Dotty. 'Hope the

feelin' lasts 'til they've gone, sweetface.'

Bad temperedly, Dotty pushed her aside, grumbling: 'You've just had your ration.'

'You can be a right arsehole, can't ya,' Liz Dotty pouted.

'We know you like hanging around children's play areas, Dotty,' Bailey began.

'I like to see kids happy. Nothin' wrong with that.'

'Depends on your idea of happiness, Dotty,' Chapps growled.

'And we also hear that you like to hang around outside schools when the pupils come out,' Bailey said.

'Me van packed in. I was waitin' for a mate to come and help.'

'And the name of this knight in shining armour?'

'Lenny Cartwright.'

'And where might we find Mr Cartwright.'

'Two doors along the hall.'

'And he'll confirm your story?'

'No reason for him not to.'

'Well rehearsed, was it?' Chapps put in. 'This alibi.'

Dotty sat up aggressively. 'This is about that kid who was filched away, ain't it? Well, I had nothin' to do with that. Or any other kiddie stuff neither. Got it.'

'Don't upset yourself, Albert,' Liz Dotty crooned. 'It's his blood pressure. Sky high, it is.'

'Try honest work to bring it down,' Chapps snorted.

Chapps's point scoring made an already bad tempered situation worse.

'Piss off. Now!' Dotty bellowed.

'Ain't right for a copper to say things like you've just said,' Liz Dotty challenged Chapps. 'Albert might have to make a complaint to your superiors, 'bout police nastiness.'

'We can't do that, Liz, love,' Dotty said.

'Why not?'

'We don't talk pig, do we.'

Liz Dotty rolled about on the couch. 'Oh, that's good, Albert. We don't talk pig.' More rolling about.

Looking about at the filthy flat, Chapps said, 'Surprising. When you live in a pigsty.'

Liz Dotty's mood changed with lightning speed to one of aggression. She sprang off the couch, spitting fire. From past knowledge, Dotty reading her intentions, stepped between them and took the slap in the face intended for Chapps. She tussled with Dotty to get past him to try again.

'Settle down, Liz,' Dotty said, his work cut out to restrain her. 'That's all they want, ain't it. You smack him, next thing we're banged up, and I'm fitted up.'

'If you've done nothing, you have nothing to worry about,' Clive Bailey said.

'Yeah,' Dotty snorted. 'Pull the other.'

Liz Dotty broke free of her husband's hold, strode to the door and yanked it open. 'Out! And don't come back.'

Bailey enquired of Dotty where'd he'd been when Miranda Watts was abducted.

'With me mate,' he replied.

'Mr Cartwright?' Chapps asked cynically.

'Yeah. Lenny and me's good mates.'

'Help each other out a lot, do you?' Bailey asked, tongue-in-cheek.

'Yeah, we do,' Dotty replied, before realizing the subtext of Bailey's question. 'Not like you think, fancy-pants! I ain't done nothin' that you should be round here givin' me and Liz grief 'bout.' Bailey thought that he might be very wide of the mark, but he was inclined to believe Albert Dotty. 'Now piss off the pair of ya!'

'Bastards,' Liz Dotty shouted after Bailey and Chapps before slamming the door shut hard enough to cause subsidence.

'Leave it,' Chapps said, when Bailey made to turn back. 'Another time, if needs be.'

Surprised by the suddenness of the conflagration spilling out of the Dottys' flat, a boy, no older than twelve or thirteen, Bailey reckoned, hurriedly withdrew the needle he was injecting himself with and fled down the stone stairs.

'Oi, you!' he called out.

Chapps again restrained Bailey, as he went in pursuit of the youngster. 'He'll only shoot up again as soon as he's out of the nick.'

'Ignoring them won't make the problem go away,' Bailey grumbled.

'Helping them might, though. Someone has to start somewhere, sometime, or we're all down the pipehole.'

'You're a copper,' Bailey said tersely. 'Not their guardian angel.'

'You know nothing about policing in a dump like this,' the PC replied hotly. 'You've been wrapped in cotton wool in the Training Division.' DC Clive Bailey knew that Chapps had been goaded into saying what everyone else had been thinking. 'The whole place should be pulled down,' Chapps went on apace. 'I've seen better animal compounds than this.'

Both men trenchant in their views, the difference of opinion went on apace.

'Namby pamby bollocks!' Bailey bellowed. He pointed to

his toecap. 'That up the backside, is all this lot will understand. And you'd be well advised, PC Chapps, to shut it now, before you're up on a disciplinary charge.'

The two men stood glaring at each other for a long time, neither of a mind to give ground. The impasse was broken by the hard-faced teenage girl, called Julie, to whom they had spoken on the way into Block 3, stepping from the lift. Quick to understand the brooding atmosphere, she chirped, 'Ain't he givin' it t'ya the way you like it then?' Her cheeky remarks were addressed to Bailey. 'Go on then, kiss and make up.'

'Exactly the person I'm looking for,' Bailey said.

'No, you ain't. 'Cause I ain't lookin' for you.' As she breezed cockily past, Chapps restrained her. 'Get your filthy mitts off me, pig!'

'We'd like you to make a statement about seeing Albert Dotty outside the school,' Bailey said.

'Wha'cha talkin' 'bout?' She looked about her vaguely. 'Where am I, eh? It's me mind, ya see. Goes completely blank. Never seen ya before.' The teenager wandered off muttering. Entering a flat further along the hall, she gave them the finger.

DC Helen Rochester listened with interest as WPC Anne Fenning relayed to her the details of Sylvia Planter's form.

'Don't keep it to yourself,' PC Brian Scuttle said, when Rochester took time to look back with renewed interest at the Planter cottage.

'Sylvia Planter was done for demanding money with menace a couple of years ago. Got community service. She had a client, a woman who longed to contact her deceased brother. When she suspected Planter's genuineness, she refused to cough up what she had agreed to pay. Planter harrassed and threatened her for several weeks, before the woman got sense and informed the police.'

'Told you,' Scuttle said boastfully. 'All this talking to the spirits lark is utter rubbish. A way to put the squeeze on the gullible and the grieving.'

Helen Rochester did not remind Scuttle how impressed, indeed how unhinged, however briefly, he had been when Sylvia Planter had mentioned his friend who had died.

'Similar scenario between Sarah Watts and Planter,' Rochester said. ''Maybe this time she went one further.'

'A big leap from demanding with menace to abduction,' Scuttle said.

'Has the room been cleaned, tidied?' Andy Lukeson enquired of Sarah Watts when she ushered them into what had been Simon Bennett's room.

'No need. Simon was a very tidy sort. His father was an army officer. Simon inherited his military gene. Everything in its place, sometimes to the point of obsessiveness. Could be quite tiresome.'

'We shan't be long,' Lukeson said.

'I hope not,' Watts said, leaving. 'Enough time's been wasted already.'

Lukeson felt like detailing the sheer slog which had already gone into finding Miranda Watts, but he knew that, convinced as Sarah Watts was that they were dragging their feet, he would be wasting his time.

Charlie Johnson closed the room door. 'She's an odd lot, isn't she, Andy.'

'She seems detached.'

'Detached? She's on another bloody planet!'

'People react in different ways to shock, Charlie. Some rant and rave. Some go off into another world. And others, not many admittedly, are like Sarah Watts. Calm and pragmatic. Inside her innards are probably knotted.'

'Bollocks! She's the original ice-maiden. Maybe we should have the house and grounds searched?'

'That would bring, if you'll pardon the pun, the house down round us. Get it wrong and its heads on the block time.'

'Would you be so careful if it was a council gaffe?'

'What're you saying, Charlie? Be precise.'

'Sorry. I'm talking out of my rear end, Andy.'

'No you're not, Charlie. You're argument is a valid one. No one should be ruled out as a suspect. I'll arrange for a search.'

'As tidy as can be, isn't it,' Johnson said, looking about the room. 'Servicing her ladyship was a more or less full-time job, I reckon. So Bennett wouldn't have spent much time in here. Just a brief rest period. Lucky sod.'

'Fancy Ms Watts then, do you, Charlie?'

'Well, she's still . . . OK.'

'Don't overdo the flattery.'

'Lots of dosh.'

'You mercenary bastard.'

'I could think of worse ways to spend my time.' Johnson's grin was vintage cheeky chappie. 'Like being a copper.'

Andy Lukeson chuckled.

The next ten minutes were spent in combing over the room with negative results. Lukeson was about to leave when he spotted a scrap of paper protruding from the end of a curtain pole. 'Give me a leg up, Charlie,' he requested. The end of the pole had a removeable cap which, when removed, revealed a hollow interior. The scrap of paper was the flap of an envelope. Lukeson inserted two fingers and retrieved the envelope secreted inside. Dropping back to the floor, he went to the bed and spread out the contents of the envelope on it.

'Bloody Moses!' Johnson exclaimed, on seeing the explicit photographs of Miranda Watts. 'Looks like our Mr Bennett's been a naughty boy.'

The photographs were of Miranda Watts in various unposed positions, Lukeson reckoned. The one which Lukeson was holding was of Miranda reaching across a picnic table, her dress riding high up her thighs. Another, even more revealing, was of Miranda sitting cross-legged on the lawn reading a book. Her demeanour in the twelve photographs in the envelope was one of a complete lack of self-consciousness, achievable only, Lukeson was sure, by a total ignorance of what was taking place. If Bennett had been the snapper, it put him in a completely different league.

'It's his room,' said Johnson, when Lukeson revealed his thinking.

'Yes. But have there been others who might have been in Watts employ?'

'Let's ask the lady of the manor, eh.'

WPC Anne Fenning complained to her errant brother who was, and not for the first time, looking for what he called SB, sibling assistance, and which she called a handout, 'The other phone's ringing. Well, you'll have to hold on, won't you,' she added narkily, when Sid Fenning moaned about having to wait. 'If I'm kicked out, sibling assistance will take a beating, won't it.' She reached for the ringing phone. 'Fenning.'

'It's Hilly,' the woman said.

'Hello, Hilly,' Fenning said, hoping that she had successfully disguised her surprise and excitement. She pressed the silent button on the phone.

'Did you arrest him?' Hilly was enquiring.

'Sammy, get a trace on this call,' she called to a colleague. 'Quickly.' Fenning released the silent button and responded, 'It takes time, Hilly.'

'Time?' she said tetchily. 'He might do it again, mightn't he.'

'I'm sure—'

'Of nothing. Put me onto someone who knows what they're doing.'

Fenning grasped the opportunity to trace the call by extending Hilly's stay on the phone.

'Well, the senior officer investigating is about,' she lied. 'Shall I fetch him to the phone, Hilly? It might take a minute or two though.'

There was silence.

'Hilly?' She looked to Sammy who shook his head to indicate that the trace had not yet been made. 'Hilly. Are you still there?'

'It's Vi,' she whispered fearfully.

'Vi?'

'Violet. She'll be furious if she catches me on the phone again.'

'We can keep you safe,' Fenning said. 'If you'll tell me where you're phoning from.' Fenning held her breath.

A bell rang in the distance.

'Someone's at the front door,' Hilly said in an urgent whisper. 'Must go.'

'We could call back.'

'Don't be ridiculous. If you phoned back, Vi would know I'd been on. Not very bright are you, for a police officer.'

The phone went dead. Fenning looked hopefully to Sammy, who shook his head.

'Shit!' Fenning groaned.

'Sis?' Fenning looked wearily at the phone her brother was on. 'What game are you playing at,' Sid Fenning groused. 'Think I have nothing better to do with my time except hang on the end of a phone.'

'Oh, shut your gob, Sid,' Fenning barked into the phone. 'Give me the number of the payphone you're calling from. I'll phone you back. And what happened to the mobile I gave you?'

'Must have left it some place.'

'Flogged it, did you?'

'Sis,' he exclaimed. 'Would I.'

'Don't bullshit me, Sid. The phone number.'

'I can't hang about.'

'You'll have to.'

'I can't. There's this bloke I owe money to. Not a nice man, sis.'

In her mind's eye, Fenning could see her brother looking shiftily over his shoulder. It did not take much to imagine. She had seen him do it so many times.

'Why do you get yourself into this sort of mess, Sid?' she said plaintively.

'Guess I can't manage very well,' he said, sad hopelessness in his voice etched in every word.

Anne Fenning regretted having been sharp with him.

116

He had proven himself a long time ago to be the addictive type. One of his addictions, probably his most destructive, was gambling. Some would say that gambling was the worst of all failings. She supposed she could not blame him. He had inherited whatever gene was responsible (and it seemed that nowadays there was a gene responsible for every human condition) from their Uncle Bert who, like Sid Fenning spent his life chasing the next win. Until one day, having put everything he had on the sure-fire winner of the 3.30 at Doncaster – which turned out to have leaden legs – he quietly ended it all before, like Sid now, the men to whom he was indebted called round to put him back in the hospital for the third time in six months.

'There's a branch of my bank near the nick. Meet me there in ten minutes.'

'This will be the last time, Anne,' he said, a promise on a promise on another promise.

Fenning went into the hall. Looking about desperately, she spotted a colleague she had dated a couple of times with no great success. He had been as glad to ditch her, as she him. But they had remained on good working terms. She hoped that now she could prevail upon him to sit in for her while she popped out. 'Chris,' she called out, hurrying after him. 'Got a minute to spare?'

'On a break. I'm on my way to the canteen. Why?'

He sounded grumpy. Not one of his better days, she reckoned. Mood swings had been a big part of why they had parted. Chris Larkin was either sky high or in the pits, and seldom anywhere in between.

'I need someone to keep my chair warm while I pop out. Won't be more than a quarter of an hour,' she added pleadingly, when he did not immediately agree to cover for her.

'There must be someone in your outfit, Anne, who can—'

'There's no one, Chris.'

'We're all stretched to the limit. It's like a bloody Stalinist Gulag!' he moaned.

She played a card she had not wanted to play. 'It's Sid.'

'In it again, is he,' he said unsympathetically.

Chris Larkin had only met Sid Fenning once, and he had expressed a desire never to meet him again. A fifty pound note, which Larkin was certain had been in the pocket of a jacket he had taken off while he watched 'Strictly Come Dancing' on the telly with Anne went missing, shortly after he had overheard Sid Fenning unsuccessfully put the touch on his sister. It had forced her to tell Chris all about her brother, pleading with him to accept the replacement note she offered. He had not done so. The incident had been the straw that had broken the camel's back.

'He'll bleed you dry, if you let him, Anne.'

'He's promised that this is the last time.'

Chris Larkin looked exactly how someone would look at an idiot.

'Go on, then. Staying away from the canteen will be good for my sugars and fats.'

'Thanks, Chris. I owe you.' She kissed him on the cheek.

He laughed. 'Is that an instalment or full payment?' His laughter, when he did laugh, which was rare, was infectious. 'Get on,' he said, when Fenning seemed lost for an answer, which in fact she was.

Sarah Watts seemed incapable of speech when Andy Lukeson showed her the revealing pictures of Miranda

Watts, which he and Charlie Johnson had found secreted away in Simon Bennett's room. 'The naturalness of the poses suggest that the photographs were taken secretly, without Miranda's knowledge,' Lukeson said by way of consolation.

'I . . . I. . . .'

'Was Bennett the only occupant of the room?'

'Yes. Since I bought it, the house has been in a constant process of being hauled into the twenty first century. Before Simon moved in, the room was full of junk and hadn't been used in an age.'

'We need to talk to Bennett urgently. You mentioned earlier that he had a bolthole in St Ives. Can you be more specific?'

'A friend has a cottage there he lets him use.'

'Name of this friend?'

'I heard Simon address him once on the phone as Hubert. Cricket pal, I think.'

'No surname?'

'No.'

'Phone number?'

'Afraid not. But I think this Hubert is local. . . .'

'Oh?'

'Simon used to dine with him reasonably often. He'd leave about eight and be home by ten to ten thirty. Couldn't have gone very far.'

'Anything else which might narrow the field?' Lukeson enquired.

'No. Simon served a purpose. I wasn't interested outside of that.'

'I need a photograph of Simon Bennett.' Lukeson let his gaze wander over the photographs in the room. There was even one of Danny Marlaux which was a surprise, after his and Watts's acrimonious bust-up. One oddity struck him. There was no photograph of Miranda Watts to be seen. He would have thought that, being an only child, Miranda would have had pride of place. It resurrected thoughts about the relationship between Sarah and Miranda Watts.

'Camera shy. Hated photographs,' Watts said. Then, ruefully: 'At least I thought he did. But I was obviously wrong. He might not have wanted to be photographed himself, but he obviously did not mind photographing other people. Bastard!'

'Description, then,' Lukeson asked frustratedly.

'A touch over six feet. Fair hair. Fair complexion. Blue eyes.' He'd have gone down well in Nazi Germany, Johnson thought. 'Has a small scar, almost faded, under his right eye where a cricket ball hit him when he was at university.'

Mention of university brought yearbooks to mind. A possible source of Bennett's photo. But, of course, in the short time between the young man of university and the older one of the workplace, great change took place, often making the younger and older man unrecognizable to those other than longtime friends.

Sarah Watts looked at the photographs which Lukeson had shown her. 'You know, despite these, I still find it hard to grasp that Simon was the kind of man these pictures would have you believe him to be.'

Leaving her in a reflective mood, Lukeson and Johnson took their leave.

'A needle in a haystack, this Hubert,' Charlie Johnson said.

120

'Maybe not, Charlie,' Lukeson said. The kernel of an idea about how he might find the man called Hubert had come to mind.

CHAPTER SEVEN

'What do you want?'

PC Jack Allington simply said, 'A word, madam,' to the hostile woman who had answered the front door of the house, the last in a long line of doors he had knocked on.

'Sorry.' Her apology was perfunctory, often given and never meant, Allington reckoned.

'Just a few brief questions, madam,' he said patiently, though at the end of an energy-sapping slog he was not of a mind to be patient or polite.

'I don't have time for chit-chat.'

'This is a police inquiry,' Allington stated starchily, his young face taking on the displeasure of a far older man. 'We'd appreciate your cooperation,' he added in what he hoped was a manner that implied involuntary if not voluntary cooperation.

Not one to be easily intimidated, Allington was beginning to think that he'd bitten off more than he could chew when, after due consideration, she relented but did not surrender. 'Come to the point quickly and be on your way.'

Only recently engaged, Allington wondered if in time

his sweet-natured bride-to-be would become a harridan like this one. He could not possibly imagine her being born such a tartar, and therefore the only explanation was that she had become such. He wondered if there was a mister. If there was, he had his unequivocal sympathy.

'We're making enquiries about an incident in Thatcher's Lot. And you'd be, madam?'

'Violet Grimes. And I don't know anything about any incident in Thatcher's Lot or anywhere else. Goodbye.'

The front door was closed in Allington's face. Grimacing, he hammered on the brass door knocker again. When the door re-opened, he said grimly, 'I hadn't finished.'

Violet Grimes, replied in an equally grim manner: 'But I had. Now it would be most ironic if I had to call the police to get rid of the police off my doorstep, don't you think?'

'Do you live alone?'

'Is that any business of yours?'

'I would remind you, madam, that your attitude could be misconstrued as obstructing a police inquiry.'

'By whom?'

'By the police,' said Allington, his tone of voice and manner saying that he had had quite enough of Violet Grimes's shenanigans.

She got the message.

'I live with my older sister.'

'May I have a word with her?'

'She's resting.'

A vase crashed to the hall floor.

'Resident ghost?' Allington said, eyebrow raised.

'Cat.' When it was obvious that the police officer did not believe her, resigned, Violet Grimes stepped aside. 'Better come in, I suppose.'

'Thank you.'

Hilda Grimes was standing stock still in the middle of the hall in a pool of flowers and water, fragments of the shattered vase from the hall table against which she had knocked scattered about. 'Sorry, Vi,' she said, in the apprehensive manner a student who had not completed his homework might with a tyrannical teacher. 'Took a bit of a wobble, I'm afraid.'

'Don't call me Vi! You know how I hate having my name abbreviated. Vi is so common, Hilly.'

Hilly.

Allington fought to contain his excitement. Wet behind the ears, and he'd struck gold. Couldn't do him any harm at all. But, of course, a little voice inside his head cautioned. There could be more than one Hilly about.

'My sister Hilda,' Violet Grimes said, with the classic hopelessness of the self-indulgent martyr. 'This police officer wants a *word*, I believe the phrase is. Why I can't imagine.'

'I shouldn't have phoned the police, Vi.'

'Violet!'

'Sorry, Vi . . . Violet.'

Hilly Grimes cowered under Violet Grimes's fury.

'You phoned the police?' she questioned, in the demeaning manner of the classic bully.

'I had to tell them about that awful man, Violet,' Hilly Grimes pleaded.

'What awful man?'

'The murderer in Thatcher's Lot.'

Violet Grimes looked starkly to PC Jack Allington for enlightenment.

'Your sister phoned in a report,' he said.

'What were you thinking of, Hilly,' said Violet Grimes angrily. 'Thatcher's Lot!'

'When I went for my walk, Violet, I went a bit off course. Then I. . . .'

She whispered to Violet Grimes, who responded, concernedly: 'That was most foolish, Hilly. Anything could have happened to you.'

'I need to know exactly what happened,' Allington said.

Violet and Hilly had another whispered conversation, after which Violet said, 'Why don't you go and make us a nice cup of tea, Hilly.' When Hilda Grimes eagerly vanished through a door, presumably the kitchen at the end of the hall, Violet Grimes told Allington of how her sister had been suffering from a bladder infection, which made it necessary for her to relieve herself frequently. 'Which she was compelled to do in some bushes. From there she saw this man standing over a little girl's body.'

'Standing over the girl's body?'

'Hilly assumed that this man had murdered the girl.'

'But she didn't actually witness murder?'

'It would appear not. But Hilly can become a little confused. And the shock of what she saw wouldn't help.'

'I can imagine,' Allington said sympathetically. 'An officer from the investigation team will want to speak to your sister.'

'She's rather upset right now.'

'Understandably so.'

'I'd best. . . .' She waved her hand vaguely in the direction of the kitchen.

'I'll let myself out.'

Just then Hilly Grimes charged out of the kitchen. 'He'll

have a bump on his head. He hit his head on the branch of a tree when he ducked down.'

'Ducked down?' Allington queried.

'A car passed on the road above. I suppose he thought he'd be seen.'

'You've been most helpful, Miss Grimes,' Allington said.

'Oh. . . . Really?'

'Yes. Very helpful indeed.'

'So kind of you to say so. You will find him, won't you?'

'I'm sure we will,' Allington reassured her.

Sarah Watts had described Georgina Adams as uptight and nervy. However, the woman who opened the door of apartment 63 in the very upmarket Moonlight Towers complex in response to Lukeson's summons with a cheery, 'Darling,' was far removed from that description.

'Sorry. I was expecting someone else. My dinner guest.'

'Detective Sergeant Lukeson. DC Johnson.'

'It's about Miranda Watts, I suppose?'

'Yes. May we come in?'

'It's a bit inconvenient right now. I was just on my way out.'

Lie.

She had just said that she'd been expecting a dinner guest. Lukeson decided not to make her aware of her gaffe. He'd hold it in reserve. Should she not realize her mistake, it would be his secret to use if and when. And should she come to a knowledge of her lie, it would unnerve her and might work in his favour.

'Been expecting us, have you?' Charlie Johnson asked.

'Well, a girl goes missing from the school. I suppose everyone gets a visit, don't they.'

'Shouldn't take long,' Lukeson said.

'Frankly, I can't see how I can help. I wasn't on duty when Miranda Watts was abducted. Off sick. I suffer these horrendous migraines. And there's nothing like teaching to give one headaches. Surely someone knew of my absence?'

Andy Lukeson was furious, but with whom he was not sure. The fault could lie with him. DI Allen was a meticulous man, so it would be unlikely that he had omitted mention of Adams's absence. Whatever happened, the end result was a copious amount of egg on his face.

'Laid low for the day, eh,' he said conversationally. 'Dark room. Curtains drawn.'

'Yes. A fellow sufferer, I see.'

'The odd time. Well, if you weren't at the school, there's nothing you can tell us. Sorry for troubling you, Ms Adams.'

'No trouble.'

'Enjoy your evening.'

'I'll try.'

Entering the lift, Charlie Johnson said, 'That was short and sweet. A tad confused about whether she was coming or going. When we arrived, she was waiting for a dinner guest to arrive. Then she was going out. Both can't be true.'

'Glad to see that you're staying alert, Charlie,' Lukeson said. 'There's CCTV at the entrance to the block. I'm betting that the footage on the day Miranda Watts was abducted, the day Georgina Adams claims she was stricken, will be revealing.'

'How can she afford an apartment in the swishest block in town on a teacher's salary?'

'Interesting question, that,' Lukeson said.

*

'Ain't got it,' said the Head of Security for the Moonlight Towers complex in answer to Lukeson's request for the CCTV footage he sought. 'Systems cock-up. Got gremlins in it. Don't tell anyone, but the camera covering the front of the complex is about as useful as a eunuch in a brothel.'

Still bemoaning his luck, Lukeson was just in time to warn Johnson, as he reversed out of parking, about the Range Rover cutting behind him at pace. 'Bloody lunatic!' Johnson swore. About to get out of the car to challenge the driver of the Range Rover, Lukeson grabbed him by the arm, nodding in the direction of the entrance to the apartment complex where Georgina Adams was hurrying to meet the driver of the Range Rover.

The man was Danny Marlaux!

CHAPTER EIGHT

'Oh, dear me,' Hilly Grimes sighed, looking about utterly confused. 'So many trees.'

'Take your time, Miss Grimes,' PC Allington said encouragingly.

Violet Grimes who had accompanied her sister, complained: 'Hilly has a weak chest. She'll catch her death here. We should go now.'

'Yes, of course,' Allington said, uncertain as to how much he could insist. Hilly Grimes was a frail woman. Should she become ill, Allington could see all sorts of problems looming, every one his. His thoughts, again, as they had been since he had graduated from police college, were of an impressive rise through the ranks; a rise that could be scuppered if he attracted the wrong kind of attention. Allington's first thoughts had been to pass the information he'd acquired up the line, but a rush of blood to the head, as he was now beginning to see his trip to Thatcher's Lot as, made him think that finding the tree on which the man whom Hilly Grimes had seen hit his head, leaving possible all-important forensics, could only speed up his progress up the ladder of promotion.

'Come along, Hilly,' Violet Grimes commanded.

'But. . . .'

'No buts about it. You'll get ill. And you're a handful enough as it is,' Violet said, with the frustration of a involuntary carer.

Allington thought about reeling off the importance of possible forensic evidence, but decided that to do so would only get Violet Grimes's back up more than it already was. He'd play it safe and take the credit which would come his way, while bemoaning the bounce his career would have got had he actually found the tree of which Hilly Grimes spoke, and could have led forensics right to it.

'It would help if you could describe this man for me, Miss Grimes,' Allington said.

'Biggish.'

'Tall, you mean?'

'More. . . .' She drew a circle round her.

'A heavy man?' Hilly Grimes nodded. 'And what did this man look like?'

Hilly Grimes became flustered. 'I didn't actually see him, you see. He had his back to me, Constable.'

'He never turned around?'

'He might have. But I hid in the bushes. I was terrified.'

'Perfectly understandable, Miss Grimes,' Allington said pleasantly. 'You could have been in great danger had he seen you. Colour of hair?'

'Dark, greying.'

'Height?'

'Oh that's difficult. He was stooped over.'

As descriptions went it was not of much value. How many overweight greying men of indeterminate height were there.

'Wait!' Allington, who was despondently leading the way out of the Lot, came up short. Hilly Grimes was going towards a stunted tree, a mix of several entangled varieties. She closely studied a low hanging branch of the tree. Then, exultantly: 'There!' She pointed. Allington joined her. 'Told you so, didn't I.' Allington was looking at a brownish stain; a stain he reckoned was dried blood. And, excitedly, what looked like a fragment of snagged skin attached to it.

PC Allington's dreams of being chief constable one day, not too far off, raced back to mind.

'Knock me down with a feather,' said Charlie Johnson. 'Danny Marlaux. What do you make of that, then?'

'What indeed,' Lukeson mumbled. 'Time for another chat, I think.' When Lukeson greeted him, Marlaux did his best to hide his surprise, but failed. It had been twenty minutes since they'd left Georgina Adams, and the expectation must have been that they'd departed, and would have had Lukeson not gone to security.

'Andy. This is a surprise.'

'I don't think so, Danny,' Lukeson said. 'I'm sure Ms Adams has brought you up to date, hence your fire brigade arrival.'

Adams became agitated. Marlaux put an arm round her to calm her. 'Let's go inside.'

Nothing was said on the way up in the lift to Adams's apartment. Once inside, Marlaux said, 'Georgie was with me that day. We were in bed together when Miranda was abducted.'

'Not the best of alibis,' Lukeson said curtly.

'Alibis?' Marlaux snorted. 'Do we need them?'

'You must have thought so, Danny. When you just gave one, unrequested.'

'What're you doing here anyway?' Marlaux asked tetchily.

'Sarah thinks Ms Adams may have played a part in Miranda's abduction.' Danny laughed derisively. 'As a vendetta against her for stealing away a man called Robert Cross, Ms Adams's former colleague and boyfriend.'

'Vindictive bitch!' Marlaux exploded. Then protested: 'That's bloody ridiculous.'

'Of course an alibi for Ms Adams, is also an alibi for you,' Lukeson said meaningfully.

'You can't be serious. Why would I abduct my own daughter?'

'Miranda is not your daughter, Danny. You told me. Remember?'

'Cheap shot Andy. Maybe not by blood, but in every other way she is.'

'I can buy that,' Lukeson said. 'I saw you together at that garden party you invited me to. It was obvious that you adored her, and she you. So to have her with you, you might—'

'This is tosh, Andy!'

'There is one other possibility. . . .'

'Oh, yeah.'

Lukeson did not want to prolong Danny Marlaux's misery, past friendship and sympathy being the primary reasons. But no one ever said that being a copper was easy.

'Know who the father is?'

'Sarah is a very liberated woman, Andy. Her lovers were legion.' He snorted. 'Not a woman to get headaches.'

'Does Miranda know?'

'Don't be daft!'

'It must have been a shock for her when you left.'

'I suppose.'

'Shock enough to have her form a bond with your replacement maybe.'

'Bennett?' His first reaction was scathing of the idea. However, on reflection his response became more measured. 'Saw them out and about. Seemed to be close. But not that kind of closeness, Andy. Sarah might be a copper-plated cow, but she'd not—'

'If she knew,' Charlie Johnson interjected.

Andy Lukeson did not tell Marlaux about the photographs of Miranda they had found secreted away in Simon Bennett's room, and how wrong he might be about their possible closeness, especially on Bennett's part.

'There is one other person who might have taken Miranda,' Lukeson said. 'Her real father. Sarah should be able to—'

Danny Marlaux's bitter laughter brought Lukeson up short. 'When I found out that Miranda wasn't mine, I asked Sarah whose she was. Her answer was, you pays your money, you takes your pick, darlin'.' Changing the direction of the conversation, he said, 'Never figured you for a policeman, Andy.'

'I never figured you as a gee-gee trainer, Danny.'

'I got lucky.'

'That's what life is all about, isn't it,' Lukeson said philosophically. 'Luck. Or lack of it.'

'Drop by for a drink some time,' Marlaux invited.

Andy Lukeson did not say yes or no, because he was not sure if a friendship which had been close could be anyway near as close again. His and Danny Marlaux's worlds had probably drawn apart; too much for that to be possible.

'If you don't mind me saying so, sir,' Johnson began. 'You don't seem unduly concerned that Miranda's gone missing.'

Marlaux turned on him furiously. 'Of course I'm bloody concerned, you idiot!'

He looked to Andy Lukeson for support and justification for his tirade, but received none. Because he had been thinking what Charlie Johnson had said.

'We'll be on our way, then.'

What was it about Danny Marlaux and Sarah Watts? How could they remain so apparently detached? Was their detachment a mechanism to ward off panic – the panic which would grip most people and overwhelm them. Was theirs the calm of false hope? The kind of hope that people cling to up to the last second, before they have to face cruel reality. His knowledge of Sarah Watts was superficial; bits and pieces gathered along the way. But he knew Danny Marlaux to be a caring sort. *Knew?* The word clanged about in Lukeson's head like a nail in an empty tin bucket. He had *known* Danny Marlaux. However, the Danny Marlaux he now knew was a long way from the Danny Marlaux of their boyhood and youth.

People changed.

Georgina Adams's bitter statement rivetted Andy Lukeson and Charlie Johnson's attention.

'If Miranda isn't found, the almighty Sarah Watts will be able to stay above water!'

Danny Marlaux shot her a malevolent look.

'What do you mean by that, Ms Adams?' Lukeson queried.

'Don't take any notice of her,' Marlaux barked. 'She's just being a bitch!'

'Oh, what's this?' Adams ranted. 'Defending the cow you walked out on? Hoping to get back in her knickers, are you, Danny?'

DC Charlie Johnson edged closer to Marlaux, ready to intervene, as judging by the purple anger in his face, Marlaux would gladly throttle her.

Obviously regretting her throat-slashing outburst, Adams said, 'Don't mind me, Sergeant. I'm just, as Danny said, being a bitch.'

'I'd still like you to explain what you meant, Ms Adams,' Lukeson insisted.

Still gripped by fury, Danny Marlaux ranted, 'Go on, then. You put in the poison. Might as well sink the dagger as well to make sure, eh.'

Lukeson concentrated his gaze on Adams, who visibly withered.

'OK, then,' Marlaux said. 'Let me. What my *former* lover. . . .'

'I said I'm sorry, Danny,' Adams whined.

'Former lover,' Marlaux re-stated, 'is referring to, is the crumbling to dust of Sarah's business empire, and how the million pounds insurance pay-out if Miranda was kidnapped would plug the financial holes.'

'Ms Watts failed to mention that,' Johnson said.

'We'll need the name of the insurance company,' Lukeson said.

'No problem, Sergeant,' Marlaux growled. 'But I might as well tell you what they'll tell you. . . .'

'And that is?'

'If Miranda isn't found within one month, seventy five

per cent of the insurance will be paid out.'

'And the remainder?'

'One month later.'

'And if after this time, for the sake of argument, Miranda turns up. What then?'

'The insurers are down a million quid. But that's the game, isn't it. It's a win some lose some business.'

'Unless, of course, they've been defrauded,' Charlie Johnson said. 'Insurance companies don't like being taken advantage of.'

Danny Marlaux held Johnson's gaze. 'That sounds perilously close to an accusation, copper.'

'Does it? I thought it was an observation. Maybe it's the way you heard it . . . sir.'

Andy Lukeson wondered why, if Sarah Watts needed financial help, Marlaux had not come to her rescue. One possible reason was that he did not have the resources to do so – he had not had a winner in a while. Or perhaps the rift between them was so wide and so bitter that had they been on the Titanic and he had the chance to save her, he would not have done so. But somehow, despite any rancour between him and Sarah Watts, Lukeson reckoned that Danny Marlaux would, if he could, have not hesitated to help Miranda. And if (Lukeson tried to put the dark thought from his mind, but as a police officer he could not) Marlaux was also in troubled waters, might they have formed a partnership to save them both from financial ruin?

Dark, murky thoughts indeed. And one more was added.

Perhaps Miranda might even have been persuaded to cooperate in insurance fraud. It would be one explanation for Sarah Watts and Danny Marlaux's apparent calm. But were one or both of them involved in a scam, would they not have been at pains to act overwrought?

A trawl through Marlaux's finances would not go amiss.

'I'm leaving now,' Danny Marlaux announced, his statement a challenge to Lukeson to detain him.

'Danny?' Georgina Adams pleaded.

'Piss off!'

He slammed the door behind him.

Adams sank into a chair and began to wail. After a perfunctory enquiry as to her well-being, Lukeson and Johnson also left.

'A million quid,' Johnson reminded Lukeson on leaving. 'Quite a motive, that.'

'Particularly if it can be collected without harming Miranda,' Andy Lukeson said darkly.

Drawing near to the station, Lukeson got a call on his mobile. Tired and disconsolate, he looked at it annoyedly. 'Yes,' he barked. 'Sorry, Anne,' he apologized immediately. He listened, his interest and excitement growing by the second. 'Kiss Allington for me. Get SOCO out to Thatcher's Lot. Tell the lab to fast-track any forensics. Oh screw that, Anne! I'll deal with CS Doyle on the overtime issue. I also want the names of recently released rapists, or would-be rapists. There was an attempted rape on Sarah Watts in Thatcher's Lot some time ago. She beat him off. Perhaps he got back at her by abducting Miranda. There's a chance that one of them might be the man we're looking for. And in your spare time,' he laughed at Fenning's response about galley slaves having better working conditions than coppers, 'run a check on Danny Marlaux's financial well-being.' He listened to more good news, and complimented

Fenning: 'You are on form. Good work, Anne.'

'Sounds like someone's brought Christmas forward,' Johnson commented wryly.

'The door-to-door found our witness from Thatcher's Lot,' he told Johnson. 'One Hilda Grimes. The man whom she saw with the girl's body ducked out of sight when a car passed on the road above. In his haste he hit his head on the branch of a tree. PC Allington, who found Hilly Grimes, took the initiative and had her go along to Thatcher's Lot. . . .'

'Cheeky.'

'They found the tree, the branch, and low-and-behold, what Allington believes is dried blood with a sliver of skin snagged in it.'

'It is Christmas,' Johnson enthused. He yawned. 'It's been a long day, eh. All fourteen hours of it.'

'Yes, it has been a long day,' Lukeson agreed. 'A good night's sleep. Fresh start.'

'A good night's sleep. I hope not. New girlfriend.'

'Anyone I know?'

Johnson chuckled. 'A copper wouldn't ask me that, guv.'

'I'll drop you off at your place.'

'No need.'

'Don't worry. I won't be staying.'

DC Charlie Johnson grinned.

'Well, in that case. Ta very much.'

Having dropped Johnson off, Lukeson thought he'd test the idea he'd had when he'd left Sarah Watts. He turned left off the roundabout at the end of the street where Johnson lived, and left again a mile on for Loston Cricket Club.

*

'Not here, I'm afraid,' was the young woman's response to Lukeson's request to speak with the club secretary. 'Portugal. Winter sunshine break.'

'Lucky Mr Cox,' Lukeson said, Cox being the name on the door of the office he'd entered, above Club Secretary. 'And you are?'

'Melanie Matthews. Phillip's . . . I mean, Mr Cox's PA.' Lukeson reckoned that Cox had a very cozy relationship with his PA. 'On his own in Portugal. Don't think I'd fancy that. But that's the bachelor life for you.' Lukeson thought that Melanie Matthews had cleverly put to rest any scandal which her earlier slip of the tongue had implied.

'Wouldn't mind a bit of sunshine meself,' Lukeson said chummily.

Melanie Matthews didn't do *chummy*.

'Mr Cox will be back in a week or so. If you'd call back then. Membership, is it?' Lukeson flashed his warrant card. 'Oh . . . I suppose not.' Obviously, in Melanie Matthew's mind, coppers and cricket did not mix. 'Can I be of help?'

'So kind of you to offer. It's about a probable member.'

'Probable member?'

'I take it you have a members list?'

'Yes. But it's not open to scrutiny.' The very prospect shocked Melanie Matthews.

'Surely not,' Lukeson said. 'Except, of course, to the police.'

'I'm not . . . you see. . . .' Melanie Matthews had gone from a state of command to one of shifting sands. 'I should have to check with Mr Cox, when he returns.'

Tired of beating about the bush, Andy Lukeson said, 'Do it now.'

'But I've told you, Mr Cox is in Portu—'

'I'm sure Mr Cox is contactable, Ms Matthews.'

'He'd hate being disturbed.'

'And I hate waiting. I'm not the patient type, you see.'

'I . . . well, perhaps, under the circumstances if you were to tell me this person's name I could help without breaching the confidentiality of the members list. Frankly, I can't imagine any member of Loston Cricket Club being of interest to the police.'

'His name is Hubert.'

'Second name?'

'Don't have it. But how many Huberts can Loston Cricket Club have?'

Melanie Matthews thought long and hard before answering: 'There is Hubert Elk. But he's a most respectable sort,' she added hurriedly.

'I'm sure he is. Not about, is he?'

'No.'

'Address?' This posed a terrible dilemma for Ms Matthews. 'I'm afraid I must insist,' Lukeson said.

'Perhaps if I phoned Mr Elk to tell him you're here?'

'Rather you didn't.'

'I shall have to check the members list.'

Elk's address (in a very posh part of Loston) in hand, Lukeson thanked Melanie Matthews for her help, paused on his way out and said, 'Like I said, I'd rather you didn't make Mr Elk aware of my visit.'

Arriving home, Andy Lukeson leaned back against the door of the flat, his gaze taking in its gloomy interior, wondering why (not for the first time) he had spent so many years in a place that he had never really liked, merely tolerated. Was it a sign of laziness on his part, apathy, lack of ambition perhaps? It would explain why he had not taken Jack Porter's job when he had quit, and why he seemed content to drift along, always the understudy, never the star. 'Someone should put a firecracker up your backside, Lukeson,' CS Frank 'Sermon' Doyle had said, in reference to what he saw as his lack of *get up and go*. 'It's not natural for a copper not to want to climb the greasy pole of promotion, laddie.' To which he had replied that not everyone wanted to be Chief Constable; that some people were very happy to reach a level they found comfortable and remain at that level. 'Utter bollocks!' had been Doyle's response.

He had dropped by Elk's house on the way back from the Cricket Club to find it empty. Just as well, he'd thought. Coppers went best in pairs.

He was undecided between watching Spurs v Liverpool on telly at home or going down to the pub and settled for remaining in. He had developed a habit of visiting his local of late which, if not checked, could easily become a bad habit.

He thought of Speckle and decided to phone her.

'Hello. . . ?' On hearing Sally Speckle's voice, Lukeson had a feeling that he was intruding. Her decision to return or not, was hers alone to make. He could not talk to her objectively, so better to say nothing at all. He went to hang up.

'Andy. . . ?'

'Ah . . . yeah. Haven't lost the instinct of a good detective, I notice,' he joked.

'Were you going to hang up just now?'

'No.'

'Liar.'

'I thought I'd be intruding,' he confessed.

'That's nonsense. There's no one better I'd like to talk to.'

'Really?' he said with childlike eagerness.

'How are things with you then?'

'So-so. More budget cuts. Less coppers to go round.'

'Nothing much changes.'

'Nothing ever changes.'

The conversation petered out in the kind of awkward impasse that occurs when those involved are frantically searching for something neutral and non-committal to say. He thought about that great English fall-back, the weather, always good to bridge an awkward gap. But Sally Speckle's laughter bubbling from the phone like liquid gold, at least to his ears, saved the day.

'Listen to us, will you,' she said. 'We sound like estranged lovers who meet up out of the blue. So say something, Andy. I'm blushing.'

'We can hardly be estranged if we never were.' He winced, and went on quickly: 'How are things in Ireland?'

Sally Speckle's laughter deepened.

'God, I wonder how many times, in hundreds of years, must one Englishman or another have asked that question. Not the best. Lots of fine soft mornings. But it's peaceful and quiet. Haven't heard a single siren since I arrived. And major crime is when some tramp nicks a couple of eggs from Farmer Brown's hen-house. It's bloody restful, Andy.'

'You sound like you're well on the road to becoming native?' he said, careful to keep his disappointment out of his voice.

'I could think of worse things.'

'Like returning to Loston?' Lukeson enquired, quietly fearful of her answer, which seemed to be taking an eternity to come.

'I'm not sure what's what yet, Andy,' she said plaintively.

Lukeson was of a mind to impress upon her the need to return – Doyle had made it clear that time was running out – but he decided against it. Sally Speckle was a mature, intelligent woman who knew the ropes, and she would be only too aware that she needed to make a decision one way or the other about her future. And were he to press the matter of time and the need to make a decision, it would only ruin the impromptu nature of his call, and probably create the impression that he was Doyle's agent rather than a friend who missed her being around.

'It'll all fall into place, I'm sure,' he said, in as casual a manner as he could manage. 'You're missed around here, you know.' It was an intensely personal statement, dressed up as a generalization. He almost personalized it, but lost his bottle. And when he heard a man's voice in the background, he was glad that he had not made a fool of himself.

'Supper's getting cold, Sally.'

'Be right there, Fergal,' she called back cheerily.

'Sorry,' Lukeson said, putting a good face on his devastation. 'You have a visitor. I'll get out of your hair.'

'No hurry, Andy.'

The diplomatic answer?

'I've got notes to review.'

'Notes about what?'

'An abduction.'

'The Miranda Watts case?'

'Yeah. You know about it?'

'We have telly over here, Andy.'

'Yeah. Right.'

'Progress?'

'A brick wall so far.'

'Sally,' Fergal called out. 'Can't keep it hot for much longer.'

The man sounded top of the mornin' Irish. And Lukeson hated him. Unfair, yes. Unjust, yes. But he still hated him.

'I've got to—'

'Yes. 'Bye, Sally.'

'You'll phone again?'

'Of course.'

He had no intention of calling again.

'Nice to hear you, Andy.'

He was tempted to say sarcastically: 'Give my best to Fergal.' But said instead: 'You, too.' He hung up quickly and made a decision. He'd go down the pub to watch Spurs v Liverpool on telly.

On reaching the pub, gloom was heaped on gloom. 'Telly's just packed in,' the landlord told him glumly, watching the crowd dwindling as they hurried away to another boozer. Soon, all that was left in the normally bustling King Charles were himself and three old duffers, two of whom were sporting scarves of Loston Rugby Club, while the third wore what looked like a regimental tie. Their dress and the brandies on the table at which they were seated, set them apart as unlikely footie fans, unless it was played with an egg-shaped ball. Lukeson left his pint of bitter unfinished and left, deciding that he'd take a walk because his interest in the match had waned and the prospect of a couple of hours in his flat alone before retiring held no joy for him. And, of course, though he was not ready to admit it to himself yet, discovering that Sally Speckle had a male . . . friend? lover? had not helped to lift his spirits.

Meandering, with no definite direction in mind, his mobile rang. He swore, because he had intended powering it off and had forgotten. He thought about letting it go unanswered, but the calling number was CS Frank Doyle's mobile. 'Lukeson,' he answered wearily.

'A bit more umphh, Andy,' Doyle said.

'Tight budgets, too few officers, and long days take their toll, sir.'

'Well your day isn't over yet, laddie.' He wished Doyle would stop calling him laddie, like a headmaster addressing a recalcitrant student. 'Samuel Curly's been found.'

'Found?' he queried, picking up the inflection in Doyle's voice, and knowing before he replied what it meant.

'Hired a car. Fitted a hose to the exhaust. You'll find the car in an alleyway alongside the old railway station.'

Doyle broke the connection, probably pre-empting Lukeson's asking why someone else could not have gone. He was not a bloody one man police force!

'What?' he growled into the mobile when it rang again. It was a none too pleased DC Charlie Johnson with old news. 'See you there,' Lukeson said, resigned.

Johnson was waiting for Lukeson at the entrance to the alley where Curly had topped himself. 'No rest for the wicked, eh,' he said, his weariness matching his guv'nor's.

'No doubt about it being suicide, I suppose?'

'None.'

He handed Lukeson a bagged suicide note which ended: God forgive me.

Walking along the litter strewn alley, Andy Lukeson, not for the first time, wondered why he had not long ago got out and earned his living in a way which did not involve death and despair all the time. Maybe, he thought, that that was the real reason for Sally Speckle having called it a day, a life lived in a world at its lowest level of human cruelty and evil was not the most attractive way of earning a living.

'Better off,' Johnson opined, when they arrived at the car. 'Can't have been fun being bipolar and given to periods of delusion and fantasy. And he had a morbid fear of authority. Coppers for example. Didn't you know?' Johnson enquired when, by his reaction, obviously Lukeson had not. 'It's there in his file.'

Lukeson was unsure if Johnson was being critical, but if he was, then he had every right to be. With Curly top of the list for Miranda Watts abduction, he should have made himself familiar with every comma and full stop in his file. Instead he had depended on memory. For someone who ratted on about proper procedure, he deserved a kick up the backside for his slackness.

'It's not always possible to get round to everything when, as the chief investigating officer, you've got more pebbles to sift through than you'd find on Brighton Beach, Andy,' Johnson said generously.

Forensic Pathologist Sid Fields, and not Alec Balson, was

in attendance at the scene which both alarmed and surprised Lukeson. He had great respect for Fields, but he had a greater respect for Balson with whom he had a convivial working relationship. Had the decision to fade out police surgeons and, therefore, Balson, been made? Surely he'd have heard. The pathologist's explanation (possibly on sensing Lukeson's disappointment) came as a relief to Lukeson. 'Alec's down with a tummy bug, Andy.' Lukeson looked into the hired Fiesta where Curly, his head sideways against the driver's headrest, looked as peaceful as a baby after mother's milk.

'Definitely suicide, then?'

'Unless I'm a lousy pathologist. Or there's the mother of all surprises waiting for me when I get him on the slab.'

'Not much for me to hang around for then,' Lukeson said.

'It would seem not, Andy. Any word on the Watts girl?'

'None.'

'Anyone standing out as a possible?'

Lukeson looked into the Fiesta at Curly. 'There had been. Now . . . back to the drawing board.'

'At least,' the pathologist nodded in Curly's direction. 'One off your list.'

'It would seem.'

'Would seem?'

'Curly was bipolar, depressive and subject to periods of delusion and fantasy. He also had a morbid fear of authority figures. Samuel Curly was a mental mess. Who know's what might have been going on in his head. Perhaps this,' Lukeson held up Curly's bagged suicide note, 'is the result of delusion? While in prison, Curly consistently protested his innocence of Katherine

147

Stockton's abduction. Might that not also be delusory? The mind protecting itself from reality. Then, released, he snatches Miranda Watts, comes face-to-face with the fact that he was and is an abductor of young children, again convinces himself that it was not he who did it, and so convinced thinks that he's about to go through the entire Stockton episode again. Fear of authority and incarceration kicks in. Can't face it, and tops himself.'

'That's pretty intense stuff, Andy,' Fields said. 'Maybe you should talk to the prison services psychiatrist.' Sid Fields's brow furrowed. 'Katherine Stockton was found alive, wasn't she?'

'Yes.'

'But by pure chance, right?'

Andy Lukeson smiled. 'DC Clive Bailey would not think you a nice man. He claims that it was sheer deductive brilliance on his part that found her.'

'Ah.' The furrow on the pathologist's brow deepened. 'If your theory is correct, Andy, and Curly did after all abduct Miranda Watts, with him dead. . . . Well, if he's secreted her away as he did Stockton, it could be a slow and painful end.'

The emaciated girl in Thatcher's Lot came to Lukeson's mind. Had she been abducted, hidden away and starved? Would Katherine Stockton have ended up the same way if Clive Bailey hadn't got lucky? His were mind-numbing thoughts. There was only one contradiction in the horrible scenario, and that was that emaciation to the degree suffered by the girl in Thatcher's Lot took time; time during which Curly was in prison. So, logically, though there may be a connection between Stockton, Watts and Curly, the girl in Thatcher's Lot had to be someone else's handiwork. Two monsters at work? The thought stunned Lukeson. But he was compelled to consider the possibility. Perverts often worked in concert. And where was Simon Bennett when Stockton vanished? Not with Sarah Watts, because Stockton's abduction pre-dated Bennett's association with Watts. But that did not mean that he was not around.

Lukeson called Charlie Johnson to him. He handed Johnson the bagged suicide note. 'Rouse a graphologist. Have this handwriting verified as Curly's. There'll be plenty on file for comparison.'

'Now?'

'Now!'

'It's close to midnight.'

'It's also close to midnight for Miranda Watts, Charlie. If she's still alive,' he added glumly.

'Have you some doubt about the note being genuine?'

'Dotting all the i's and t's, Charlie.'

'Like a good copper should.'

'Right. And also arrange for another search of Curly's flat. Now, also.'

'You're going to be a popular fellow, guv.'

Johnson dispatched, Andy Lukeson turned his attention back to Sid Fields who was getting into his car to depart. 'I haven't had your full report on the girl in Thatcher's Lot.'

'You're not the only outfit on tight budgets,' Fields grumbled. 'Which makes for slower progress.' Lukeson was not at all sure that, should Alec Balson be replaced with Fields, his working relationship with the forensic pathologist would come anywhere near being as pleasant and harmonious as it had been with the police surgeon.

Fields was a careful man, never one to guess, not given to discussion until he had done all the groundwork and reached a definite outcome. Balson on the other hand was always willing to put his head on the block. His scene-of-crime opinions, and the reliability of his conclusions had more than once kick-started an investigation in those all-important early hours. 'But I have no reason to contradict Balson's findings,' Fields said formally. 'Natural causes, brought on by an asthmatic attack.' Fields frowned thoughtfully. 'And I think that Balson is probably right that fear or anxiety played their part in inducing the attack. But, as always, nothing taken is definite until my final report. OK?' A cautious, sometimes nervous man, it was what Fields always said. Walking away, Lukeson paused and turned to Sid Fields on his summons. 'Should the powers that be decide to ditch Alec Balson, I won't be filling his shoes.' He smiled. 'Why do I get the feeling that you're relieved.'

'Nothing personal. I've gotten use to Alec Balson.'

'Alec is easy to get used to. I'll miss him. I'm not sure that I'll like America. But if I want my marriage to an American woman to last, which I do, then I see no alternative but to join her there. Angela has never taken to Loston. To England. Misses the Californian sun. Goodnight.'

' 'Night.'

Andy Lukeson looked after Fields's departing car, feeling that he was in the middle of a whirlpool of change: Speckle. Balson. Fields. The only thing that remained certain was, of the three, the one who mattered the most.

DI Sally Speckle.

CHAPTER NINE

At the best of times, rendering an account of one's stewardship to CS Frank 'Sermon' Doyle was not joyous, but on this morning it was positively glum. Samuel Curly had topped himself. The suicide note had been confirmed as being in his handwriting. The prison psychiatrist had opined that Curly had indeed been innocent of Katherine Stockton's abduction, which meant that her abductor had gone unpunished and was, if the devil hadn't claimed him, still on the loose. It would not take long for the story about Curly's probable wrongful conviction and imprisonment to become known, followed by the inevitable and justified criticism of the police, and the questioning of their ability to now find Miranda Watts and bring her abductor (which, of course, would be the real culprit who should have been convicted and imprisoned in place of Samuel Curly) to book. The psychiatrist had also damningly opined that Curly's suicide had likely been the end result of his false imprisonment, which had taken his fear of authority, already acute, to the extreme and had become the catalyst for disaster when Miranda Watts had been abducted, stoking his fear of being, again, falsely accused. It gave

Andy Lukeson no pleasure at all to have been the one who had raised such a scenario early on.

'A bloody disaster!' was now Doyle's assessment of the situation.

'A bigger disaster still for Samuel Curly,' Lukeson could not prevent himself saying.

Doyle glared at Lukeson, but with a world weary sigh, concurred with him. 'In no time at all, the press will be camped out on our doorstep. There'll be hell to pay,' he warned darkly. 'And what's this hokum about Sarah Watts?'

'Mothers have harmed their children before, sir. And there's Sylvia Planter's talk about Sarah Watts's dislike of her daughter.'

'Planter is a charlatan, Lukeson. You don't believe in that contacting the dead rubbish, do you?'

'Frankly, I haven't an opinion either way, sir. But it is a fact that Miranda's arrival heralded the end of Sarah Watts's career as a model. At the time, in an interview she gave to a gossip magazine—'

'Frightful muck, gossip magazines.'

'. . . Sarah Watts indicated that Miranda's birth was at best inconvenient, and at worst a calamity. So when Planter says that she got negative vibes when Miranda was mentioned she might be on the right track. And, in a way, Miranda might also have caused her marriage to flounder.'

Doyle raised a quizzical eyebrow.

'Miranda Watts is not Danny Marlaux's child. Lots there for Sarah Watts to see Miranda as a jinx. And there's the possibility that Sarah Watts and Danny Marlaux might be acting in concert.'

'In it together?' Doyle said disbelievingly.

His look had Lukeson questioning if he'd sprouted horns. He went on to tell Doyle about Watts's financial woes and Marlaux's sinking fortunes – Fenning's trawl through Marlaux's financial state had indicated as much – and the potential for rescue in Miranda's kidnap insurance. 'The insurance payout could mean the difference between swimming clear or going under for either or both.'

Doyle was openly sceptical.

'I don't know. Abducting their own child, even to stave off ruin.'

'Maybe they didn't actually abduct Miranda, sir.'

'All these circles within circles are making me dizzy, Lukeson.'

'What if Miranda Watts, to help out, agreed to be part of the insurance scam? That right now Miranda Watts is sitting cozy someplace until the insurance company coughs up. Financial trouble over, Miranda, suitably worse for wear to allay any suspicions that all might not be as it seemed, miraculously turns up, a well rehearsed yarn to spin. Or, stage managed, spotted out of the blue and the euphoria overrides all else.'

'That, Lukeson,' Doyle said, 'is the daftest thing ever. Or an insight of Holmesian brilliance. And Planter?'

'Don't rate her,' Lukeson said.

'She's no innocent. I hope you won't end up with egg on your face, Andy. Dotty?'

'More to my liking,' Lukeson said.

'Having the Watts home and grounds searched won't be kept quiet for long.' Doyle was not criticising his decision. But he was questioning its timing.

'I considered that if we were looking at any possible

involvement by Sarah Watts, that wisdom now would be better than foolishness later, sir.'

'The media will make much of it. And your friendship with Marlaux. Much could be made of that.'

'More were friends, sir, rather than are friends. Our worlds diverged a long time ago.'

'So long as there's no exploitable conflict of interest.'

'If there were, I'd be the first to step down, sir.'

'Now Bennett's pal, this fellow Hubert something or other. . . .'

'Elk, I believe, sir.'

'Run him to ground, have you?'

'I think so.'

Lukeson told Doyle about the cricket connection between Bennett and a man called Hubert, Sarah Watts had told him about. 'I went along to Loston Cricket Club on the off chance. The club has one Hubert Elk as a member.'

'Crafty,' Doyle complimented.

'I'll be dropping by Elk's later.'

'Good. And finally, Adams. What do you think, Andy?'

'She lied about her wherabouts at the time Miranda Watts disappeared. Said she was at home ill. But when Marlaux turned up, it transpired that they were together at the time.'

'The games the rich play, eh. Watts pinches Adams's boyfriend. And Marlaux ends up in Adams's bed. A balancing of the scales, you might say. Adams and Marlaux's alibis are pretty worthless as alibis go, seeing that one or both could be up to their necks in this mischief.

'Now, about this girl in Thatcher's Lot, Andy. If there's too much on your plate I can assign someone else.'

154

'No, sir. I can manage.'

'Sure?'

'If I can't, I'll let you know.'

'Finding Watts is our priority, you understand. Any link between the girl in Thatcher's Lot and Miranda Watts, you reckon?'

'Nothing as yet.'

CS Frank 'Sermon' Doyle held Lukeson's gaze. 'Still confident you'll find Watts, Andy?'

Aware (by the morning coverage of the Watts abduction) of the honeymoon period with the media having come to an end, Lukeson had expected the question – the only imponderable was when Doyle would ask it.

'All I can do is my best, sir.'

Doyle's shift of eyes away from him told Andy Lukeson that it was not the kind of gung-ho response the Chief Super had been seeking. He could understand Doyle's unease. If he had called it right and Lukeson succeeded, back-slapping all round would be the order of the day. However, failure on his part would be placed squarely on Doyle's shoulders. Like any other organization, in the police, success was mercurial. One wrong call and one's standing slipped, sometimes, depending on the severity of one's misjudgement, never to be recovered. All it took to bring a career to a standstill, or worse, into a spiral of slow decline, was a cock-up of noticable degree. And finding a dead Miranda Watts, or not finding her at all, would be that kind of cock-up.

The media, who had given room, were now reverting to form, questioning police competence, or rather their incompetence based on their apparent inability to find Miranda Watts. No one had yet raised the possibility of

her being dead, but that would not be far off. One of the
newspapers (not a scurrilous tabloid this time, but a
respected broadsheet) had a picture of Andy Lukeson
getting out of his car in the station carpark with the
caption: IS THIS THE MAN TO FIND MIRANDA? The
story questioned police wisdom in appointing a mere
detective sergeant to lead the hunt for Watts – all mention
of his success in the Blake murder, which had initially
been given prominence, set aside – speculating that more
progress might have been made had a more senior rank
been given the task.

'Went for the bloody jugular, didn't they,' Doyle said,
taking the relevent newspaper from his desk drawer.
Though his demeanour was one of empathy, his concern
was personal, Lukeson believed. And for that he could not,
or did not blame Doyle. Sitting on a possible wrong call in
his choice of officer did not make for comfort.

Miranda Watts's disappearance had come only six
weeks after the as yet unsolved murder of a woman called
Gloria Swann, a crack cocaine addict whose body had been
found in a skip, head bashed in. Progress in the search for
her killer had ground to a halt. At the time of her murder,
Swann, due to her lowly social status, had not got much
media attention, because at the time another European
financial crisis loomed. Now Gloria Swann was being used
as a stick with which to beat the police. Doyle had much
to worry about. Because the coming together of events
could easily turn into a witch hunt.

'Maybe the upcoming press conference with Sarah
Watts might make a difference,' he said, more in hope
than certainty.

Not wanting the proverbial beating about the bush,

Andy Lukeson decided that straight talking would be best all round.

'I'll step aside if that's what's needed,' he said. 'I never wanted the job in the first place, sir.'

Doyle made supportive noises, but his relief that the suggestion of his possible replacement had been raised by Lukeson himself was obvious. 'Won't come to that, I'm sure, Andy,' he said with false cheeriness.

It had been Lukeson's intention to let doors open for both their comfort zones, but he suddenly tired of subterfuge. 'Why don't I make it easy for all concerned and request re-assignment right now, sir. There must be something simple for me to do. Something that doesn't require too much upstairs.'

Gloves off, CS Frank 'Sermon' Doyle's frown was thunderous. 'Cut out the bloody self-pity, Lukeson. Put yourself in Miranda Watts's place. You'd not thank us if we dragged our heels by leaving someone in situ who was not making progress. For now, you're still in charge. So if you don't like the idea of being booted, shift your backside off that chair and find Miranda Watts. No one will do you any favours!'

Lukeson was leaving when Doyle said:

'It's not what I'd want, Andy. You can believe that, or chose not to believe it. However, if you don't make progress soon, I'll recommend it.'

'Can't be fairer than that, sir,' Lukeson said genuinely.

'What's this in Rochester's report about Planter's estranged daughter. . . ?'

'A longshot,' Lukeson said.

'Worrying. The number of longshots in this case,' Doyle grumbled.

'Her young lad knew Miranda Watts. So maybe Ms Tompkins might have heard something. Like I said—'

'A longshot,' Doyle groaned. 'Tompkins?'

'Yes. Planter adopted the girl. When things got sticky between them, she reverted to her own name. Johnson will go round this morning to interview her.'

'Why Johnson? And not Rochester?'

'I have this theory that women react badly to other women questioning them, and more favourably to men.'

'Johnson's no oil painting, is he?'

'Something to do with biology in its more basic form, I expect, sir.'

'Don't forget the press conference. Brush up before you face the lens and pencil brigade. Although the perspiration of effort on the brow will, of course, be welcome. And be on time!' Lukeson was closing the door when the CS said, 'Good luck, Andy.'

'And won't I bloody need it,' Lukeson muttered.

'A copper can't have enough of it,' Doyle said. He grinned. 'Always had good hearing, Sergeant.'

'Shit!' Lukeson grunted, door closed firmly behind him.

CHAPTER TEN

'Nice,' DC Helen Rochester commented on the very impressive Edwardian house set in spectacular gardens. 'Not short of a bob, our Hubert.' On the doorstep, an aged Persian cat, its once luxuriant coat now shedding, was scratching on the front door to be let in, a familiar routine judging by the markings on the door.

'Should have saved me pennies,' Rochester said. 'Blinds down, curtains drawn. Looks like there's no one home.'

Five minutes later, after several summons on a bell that chimed Greensleeves, with no response forthcoming, Lukeson stepped back to look up at the house and addressed Rochester in a carrying voice. 'As you said. No one home. Best be off and not waste valuable time.' He indicated to Rochester to follow him. Getting into the car which Rochester had parked across the entrance, they drove off out of sight to park just beyond the entrance. Using a high hedge as cover, Lukeson got out and edged up to the entrance. A heavy set man was letting the cat in. *Biggish*. Hilly Grimes's description of the man in Thatcher's Lot came to mind.

'Mr Elk?' he called out, stepping into view. Although

some distance away, there was no mistaking the effect Lukeson's appearance had on the man. Lukeson was chuffed. His gamble of pretending to leave had paid off handsomely. 'DS Lukeson, sir. Wonder if I could have a word.'

'Sarge!' Sergeant Larry Getts of uniform, who was leading section A of a wider search party, looked to a small wooded area atop a hill from which a young PC had excitedly emerged. 'Up here.'

At forty-nine, overweight, and not used to being on active duty, Getts climbed the hill and followed the PC into the trees, not appreciating one little bit the effort it took. 'Wait up, Myers,' he called, when the pace set by the young PC became too much. 'What's got you so excited anyway?'

'This and that,' he said, pointing.

Getts swore.

'Mr Hubert Elk?' Lukeson enquired of the shaken man to verify the man's identification.

Sensing trouble, Judaslike, the cat leaped out of Elk's arms and sought refuge inside the house. Elk painstakingly began to brush the cat's hairs from the cardigan he was wearing, obviously a ploy to give him time to think.

Lukeson was having none of it. 'I think it best if my colleague and I stepped inside, Mr Elk.' Not waiting for an answer, he continued: 'Hurt your head, have you, sir?' Thinking that one gamble had paid off, Lukeson had decided to try his luck again. In a reflex action, Elk's hand went to the right side of his head to a point under his thick dark hair. Pity he could not so instinctively pick the lottery numbers, he thought. On a roll, he added: 'We need to ask you about an incident in Thatcher's Lot, Mr Elk. And your association with one Simon Bennett.' Panic raced through Elk with the swiftness and intensity of a bushfire driven by strong winds. Other than sound and intuitive investigative ability, Lukeson knew that to be a successful copper required luck in dollops, and had he just had a dollop of the elusive commodity. 'I think it best if we had our chat at the station, sir.' Hubert Elk put up no resistance and offered no protest. Escorting him to the waiting car, Lukeson's mobile rang. He waited to answer until Elk was in the car. Lukeson listened to Sergeant Getts brief but shattering message, and then said miserably, 'I'll be right there, Larry.'

'Miranda Watts?'

'You've heard she's been abducted, Ms Tompkins?' enquired DC Charlie Johnson, recognizing the angry woman who had stormed out of Sarah Watts's morning room.

'You'd have to have been on the moon not to have heard. What's it got to do with me?'

Johnson's nose curled at the smell of perspiration emanating from the track-suited Tompkins, who had obviously just arrived back after a very vigorous jog cross-country, judging by the muck on her trainers, which she did not have any compunction about dirtying the off-white carpet with. She was, Johnson noted enviously, an extremely well-toned and fit woman. He became aware of the extra pounds he had recently put on, nothing spectacular, but he still sucked in his tummy.

'I believe you know Miranda and Sarah Watts? Your mother—'

'If you mean that old witch Planter,' Linda Tompkins snorted bitterly. 'She isn't my mum. Never came near to being. Better off for both of us if she'd never adopted me. Did she tell you that all I was, was a replacement for her own precious tyke, who'd broken her neck because of that bitch's stupidity. What did she tell you anyway?'

'She told us that Miranda Watts and your son were good friends,' Johnson said.

'What of it?'

'We thought that Miranda might have said something,' Charlie Johnson said vaguely.

'Such as?'

Linda Tompkins was going to fight him all the way. So much for Andy Lukeson's guff about a male officer making better progress with a female.

'We were hoping that you'd recognize the significance of anything she might have said, relative to her going missing.'

'She said she hated her mum. Is that significant?'

'Did she say why?' Johnson asked.

'Not in as many words. I think it was to do with her mum's in-house stud. A man called Simon something-or-other. When Sarah turfed him out, Miranda was upset, very upset.'

'Did Miranda say why she was so upset?'

'Not specifically. But it was obvious she liked him. And I think she thought that her mum had got rid of him because of that. Danny Marlaux had upped and left. Got sense at last, I'd say. So I think ... Bennett, Simon Bennett, that was his name, became Miranda's dad in a way. And Sarah Watts isn't a sharer.'

'Meaning?'

'She's possessive. Jealous. Doesn't like competition. She likes exclusive possession. I'd say that she was well rid of Bennett. Met him once. Didn't like him.' Tompkins gave a little shiver. 'Creepy, up close. Know what I mean?'

'Is Arthur still hanging round? That old witch Planter's heavy. At it like rabbits. Disgusting at their age. But I suppose they suit each other. When the morons who believe her mumbo jumbo get sense and refuse to cough up, good old Arthur puts the squeeze on them. Not finnicky about how he makes a quid.'

Charlie Johnson wondered if making a quid included abduction.

'You seem to know a great deal about Ms Watts and Mr Marlaux.'

'All came out in the wash, didn't it.'

'Wash?'

'Yeah. Right now I'm working on a book about Napoleon.' Charlie Johnson looked vague. 'I'm a writer,' she explained, and then amended: 'Well, will be a writer. Despite that carping cow's messing me about.'

'You mean your mum?'

'No,' Tompkins said petulantly. 'Ms high-and-mighty Sarah Watts. She let me think that I could write a book about her. I spent hours on research. Then the bitch told me that if a book was written about her, it wouldn't be by an amateur hack. She's a precious cow! How a nice kid like Miranda popped out of the dragon lady, I'll never know. Must take after Danny Marlaux, I reckon. Now, if you don't mind. . . .' Linda Tompkins undressed to panties and bra. 'Shower.' She went to undo her bra, leaving

163

Johnson with no alternative but to leave.

'Do you reckon that Miranda Watts might have been fond enough of Bennett to have gone off with him, Ms Tompkins?' he asked over his shoulder on his way out.

'She might be. But I doubt very much if he'd have her along.'

Recalling the photographs which Lukeson and he had found in Bennett's room, Charlie Johnson was inclined to disagree.

DS Andy Lukeson held up the bagged blood-stained child's shoe which Getts had handed him – a girl's shoe. The match of the shoe found in Cherrytree Lane when Miranda Watts had been abducted. The little wood was not far from the Watts house. In fact the house was clearly visible from it. He looked to where the earth had been very recently disturbed, his spirits low. 'Best see what we've got?' he said glumly.

'Bad luck, that,' Getts said, indicating the bagged shoe. 'The killer must have dropped it.'

The killer.

Obviously Getts had made up his mind about what would be found under the patch of recently disturbed earth.

'Slowly,' Lukeson cautioned. 'And keep the earth in a nice neat mound close by. We don't want to lose any forensics.'

Ten minutes later, the contents of the shallow grave revealed, Getts said, 'A strange lot.' Lukeson agreed. The grave contained a doll with the name MIRANDA written on it in capital letters in what Lukeson believed was blood. The doll's neck was twisted. The grotesqueness of the discovery filled him with foreboding.

'I want a fingertip search of the wood and the surrounding area,' he told Getts. 'Every inch is to be covered. Not a sliver of forensics is to be lost.' He looked to the increasingly cloudy sky. 'And make it snappy. Looks like rain's on the way.' He handed back the bagged blood-stained shoe. 'Get this to the lab.' His sigh was long and weary. 'I expect the blood will match Miranda Watts.'

CHAPTER ELEVEN

On his way to the interview room where Elk was waiting to be questioned, Lukeson crossed paths with WPC Anne Fenning who handed him a folder. 'Completed pathology on the child found in Thatcher's Lot, guv.'

'Social Services come up with an ID? I'm sure she must have come to their attention.'

'Short staffed, they say.'

'Aren't we all,' he said sourly.

'Maybe something will come of the newpaper and telly pictures of the poor mite.'

'Don't hold your breath, Anne. This country is getting as civilly crippled as America. Hear nothing. See nothing. Know nothing. Start a fire under Social Services,' he ordered brusquely, continuing on to the interview room further along the hall. Conscious of his less than corteous manner, Lukeson paused to compliment Fenning on her contribution to the overall investigation, but she had gone. He made a mental note to do so later, and also to give her a more hands-on role next time round. She had not said, but he sensed she felt undervalued and would prefer to be more actively a part of the team. He gave a quick perusal of Sid Fields's report, his eye honing in on an underlined section. He turned and went back along to find Fenning. 'Anne. Get Animal Welfare over to Elk's house to collect his cat.'

No one spoke when Andy Lukeson entered the interview room, his mood grim. He went and sat facing Elk. Helen Rochester switched on the tape machine. Before beginning the interview, Lukeson noted the details of time, those present, and the purpose of the interview.

'What's the name of the dead child you dumped in Thatcher's Lot, Mr Elk? We have a witness who saw you dump the child's body.' He had taken a little liberty with what Hilly Grimes had stated, which was that she saw Elk standing over the body, which was not as incriminating as dumping the body. A plausible argument could be made that Elk had simply come upon the body rather than having dumped it. If that were to be his response, the inevitable question, of course, would arise as to why, having found a body, he had not reported the matter to the police. To which the answer could be that he had panicked. Under the circumstances, panic could be validly claimed. Initially, Elk had seemed ready to capitulate. Now he seemed more relaxed. Lukeson wondered to what degree Elk had gathered his wits during the necessary delay when he had had to respond to Larry Getts's summons. He worried that having put the interview on hold, he had lost the advantage of shock. Had he given the go-ahead to Rochester to begin the interview, Elk would not have had time to settle as he obviously had. He hoped that it was a mistake that he would not pay dearly for.

'Would you be prepared to take part in an identity parade, Mr Elk?'

Lukeson was again gambling on his luck being in. Hilly Grimes had not got a clear enough look of Elk to pick him out in a line-up. A clever brief would not take long to establish doubt.

'Line-ups are for criminals. I'm not a criminal.'

'What have you got to fear, Mr Elk?' Helen Rochester asked. 'If, as you say, that you are not the man this witness saw, then surely it's in your interests to have this whole matter cleared up as soon as possible.'

'I'll not take part in something, when I'm not guilty of anything.'

'Should you continue to resist our request, I believe we have sufficient grounds to insist, Mr Elk.' The change in Elk's demeanour was barely noticeable. But slight that it was, Lukeson reckoned that he had him on the run. 'Why did you try to hide in your own home, when we called, Mr Elk?'

'Hide? I wasn't hiding. I don't encourage visitors. I'm a very private person. Nothing wrong with that, is there?'

'Not in the least,' Lukeson said. 'I put it to you that you knew that DC Rochester and I were police officers. And that you did not wish to engage with us. Why was that, Mr Elk?'

'Police officers. How would I have known that. Plain clothes.'

'I put it to you that you were expecting us,' Rochester said.

'That's pure supposition.'

'How did you injure your head, Mr Elk?' Lukeson asked.

'Silly of me. Collided with the mantel, bending to stoke

the sitting-room fire.'

'So if we send forensics officers to examine the mantel we should find traces from your injury?'

'Don't think so.'

'Oh?'

'I washed it clean. It would hardly be fitting or hygenic had I not done so.'

'I don't believe you, Mr Elk,' Lukeson stated bluntly.

'Your choice, Sergeant.'

'I believe you got the injury when you struck your head on a tree in Thatcher's Lot, when attempting to hide from a motor vehicle which passed on the road above the Lot.' Elk shiftily averted his gaze. Lukeson sensed that, if played right, Elk was there for the taking. 'What's the girl's name? And why did you kill her?'

The blunt and direct accusation acted like an electric shock on Elk.

'Kill her? I d-d-didn't k-kill her.'

'I think you did,' Lukeson barked, giving no quarter. 'What was the girl's name?'

'I don't know what you're talking about.'

Elk had regained a little ground, but it was shaky.

'We'll need a DNA sample.'

'For what reason?'

'To prove that you were in Thatcher's Lot.' Hubert Elk swallowed hard. 'We've recovered forensics from the tree on which you struck your head. I believe that your DNA sample will match what we've recovered.

'I also believe that the cat hairs found in the girl's respiratory system and lungs, will match your cat's hairs.' Lukeson held Elk's gaze. 'I think it would be wise to reconsider your position.'

'I didn't kill her,' Elk said finally, after a lengthy weighing up. He slumped in his chair, all fight gone out of him. 'I haven't slept a wink in days. In fact weeks.' He wasn't getting any sympathy from Andy Lukeson. 'When she took poorly, they forced me to keep her in my home. She seemed to be improving. Enough to play with the cat. She'd hold him up to her. No one told me that she was an asthmatic,' he whined. 'I'd never have let her near the cat had I known. I did everything I could to help her. . . .'

'Except call a doctor,' Lukeson said. 'Or take her to A&E.' His contempt for Elk was absolute.

'How could I explain who the girl was. And what would those awful people do to me.'

'So you let the girl die to save your own skin. Who are they?'

'I'm an addict, Sergeant. Cocaine. Hopelessly dependent. An expensive habit. The past year has seen me get into dire financial straits. It's a familiar story. In desperation I borrowed unwisely from the wrong people, fooling myself that my indebtedness would be temporary, that I could overcome my problem and get back to normality.'

Hubert Elk hunched his shoulders miserably.

'No one is as effective a liar to oneself as an addict. Unable to meet my repayments, the people to whom I owed, came up with what they termed a payment plan. I would provide accomodation in a property I owned, for them to use as a studio for modelling shoots. At the time it seemed an ideal arrangement. Until I discovered that the models were children, and the shoots were pornographic. . . .'

Lukeson grimaced at Anne Fenning's ill-timed inter- ruption, when it looked likely that Elk was about ready to spill every bean in the tin. The name she whispered rang a bell. When she left, Elk continued, eager now to unburden himself.

'At first it was completely hands off, but not for long. I was to play a more active part. At first I refused, but my resolve crumbled. A couple of days and my craving overcame all my inhibitions and morals. Over the next couple of weeks I sank more and more into the quagmire of degradation, until Mrs Cracken phoned. . . .'

'Mrs Cracken?' Lukeson asked.

'They call her a housemother. A fanciful name for a gaoler. I was to take this sick child into my home until she got better. I had no choice. These people do not take no for an answer, Sergeant.'

'I'll need names?' Lukeson said.

'I don't know any names. Just voices on the phone.'

'Numbers you phoned back then.'

He shook his head. 'They were always very careful not to let their number be displayed.'

'How many children were involved?'

'I visited the studio, as they called it, only once. I counted ten.'

'Do you still maintain that you don't know the name of the child you . . .' Lukeson's mouth twisted sourly. 'Took care of?'

'Sally. That's all. It's what Mrs Cracken called her when she phoned.'

'Do you know a woman called Gloria Swann?'

'No.'

'She was also an addict. Crack cocaine. Where is this studio?'

'Landis Street.'

Andy Lukeson's heart leaped. Copper Alley, where Gloria Swann's body had been found, was off Landis Street.

'Six weeks ago, a young woman's body was found in Copper Alley in a skip.' There was a new pallor on Hubert Elk's face. 'Toxicology confirmed the presence of crack cocaine. Her name was Gloria Swann.'

He held Elk's gaze.

'The name of the child found in Thatcher's Lot, has been confirmed by Social Services as Sally Swann, whose mother, due to her addiction, could not adequately care for her. But before they could act, Sally disappeared. Then her mother Gloria was found murdered close to the place where her daughter was kept imprisoned. Fortunately, the scene-of-crime at Copper's Alley provided good forensics. Forensics which I believe will match those found in Thatcher's Lot, Elk.'

Hubert Elk groaned like a wounded animal.

'I didn't know who she was. But the one night I went to the house, when I was leaving this woman approached me and told me that she knew what was going on, and that she was going to the police, that I'd go away for a long time. I lost my head. I pulled her into Copper Alley and tried to reason with her. But she wouldn't listen. Then she saw a squad car and said that she'd stop it, tell them, and I was for the high jump. I smashed her head against the skip and heaved her into it. I didn't kill her intentionally. I didn't know that she was dead until I read it in the morning paper.'

'We'll need signed statements,' Lukeson said.

Elk made no objection. In fact he seemed anxious to have it all over and done with as quickly as posssible now.

172

Signed statements secured, Lukeson raised Miranda Watts.

'I had nothing to do with that,' Elk said with a weary resignation. Andy Lukeson placed a photograph of Miranda Watts before him. 'I've seen her picture in the papers.'

'Have you ever seen her at the studio?'

'No.'

'You're sure about that?'

'I've never seen her,' Elk reaffirmed.

With nothing to lose and facing a lengthy prison term (even if the Crown Prosecution Service accepted manslaughter on the grounds that Gloria Swann's killing was unpremeditated), Andy Lukeson was of a mind to believe Hubert Elk when he said he knew nothing about Miranda Watts. But there was still Elk's friendship with Simon Bennett to be considered. 'I believe you are friendly with a man called Simon Bennett?'

His sigh was that of a dying man's last breath.

'Knowledgeable. When I had money, he advised me.'

'You let him have the use of a cottage you own in St Ives. In fact it was expected he might have gone there when his relationship with Sarah Watts ended.'

'He might have. He has a key. He always went to the cottage when, as he put it, he needed to rest from his libertine ways.'

'Know him well, do you?'

'We shared rooms at university.'

'Intimate. Sharing rooms. You'd get to know a body well, sharing.'

'You think he went off with Miranda Watts, don't you?'

'Simon Bennett is a gigolo,' Elk said. 'Not a paedophile.

He specializes in women who are past causing male hormones to race. He let's them think they still can. Said women are very grateful and very generous.'

Lukeson placed one of the photographs of Miranda Watts which they had found in Bennett's room before Elk.

'This, and many more, were found in Bennett's room at the Watts house.'

Elk was genuinely stunned.

'You never suspected he might—?'

'No!'

'Other than your cottage in St Ives, do you know of any other hideaway Bennett might have use of?'

Elk shook his head.

'It seems to me that you know very little about such a good friend, Elk.'

'Look, when we left university, we went our separate ways. Didn't stay in touch. It was only about a year ago that we ran into each other again. In between there were many years of which I know nothing.'

Reckoning that there was nothing more to be gleaned, Lukeson charged Elk with the murder of Gloria Swann. The disposal of Sally Swann's body and complicity in her death. And involvement in child pornography. Hubert Elk hung his head and wept bitterly. Out of shame and remorse? Or that he had been caught? Lukeson wondered. He didn't much care. Either way, he did not have any sympathy for Elk.

'Good work, Andy,' Helen Rochester complimented when the formalities of custody were concluded.

'Thanks,' he said glumly. 'But we're no nearer finding Miranda Watts. Cuppa?'

'Could do with something a whole lot stronger, but a

cuppa will do for now.'

Ten minutes later, nibbling on a sticky bun that was proving as appetizing as cold cabbage, Helen Rochester said, 'What if Sylvia Planter has. . . .' She shifted uneasily under Andy Lukeson's intense scrutiny. *'Powers.'* Then, in for a penny, in for a pound. 'Mediums have been used by the police before.'

'But not mediums who were suspects,' Lukeson said. 'If Planter is up to her eyeballs in Miranda Watts abduction, she could lead us a merry dance.'

Rochester was not ready to let it go.

'OK. Let's say that Sylvia Planter had plans to abduct Miranda Watts, how could she be sure that Sarah Watts would pick up a magazine off a park bench, read her advert, decide that a seance for her business friends might add spice to an otherwise dull evening, and contact her? That's not a plan, Andy. Too many imponderables. How could Planter be sure that Sarah Watts would walk in the park on that day? And pick the bench she did to sit on to find the mag which Planter had left to be found. Like I said, too many imponderables.'

'Might not be such a mystery after all,' Lukeson said. 'Darren Tompkins and Miranda Watts were friends. And Linda Tompkins is Sylvia Planter's adopted daughter. . . .'

'They have nothing to do with each other, Andy.'

'Who says?'

'Tompkins and Planter,' Rochester said reflectively. Then: 'I don't think it's an act, guv. Not having seen the venom in Planter towards Tompkins. And vice versa Charlie Johnson says.'

'Might be interesting to find out if Sarah Watts is a creature of habit. I suspect she might be.' Lukeson phoned

Watts, asked his questions, got his answers, thanked her and hung up. 'Takes every Wednesday morning off, come what may, walks in the park and always sits on the same bench, which is exactly half way. And she had given a recent interview in which she expressed a curiosity about spiritualism. I think you deserve another sticky bun as a reward, DC Rochester.'

'If it's OK with you, make that a double brandy when all of this is sorted, Andy. Another thing. . . .'

'Oh, yes.'

'Miranda's real father. What if he's taken her back?'

'If he's of that mindset, why wait? She's nine years old.'

'Maybe he wasn't around.'

'Prison?'

'Or abroad. Thing is, Andy. If Marlaux only found out a while ago that he was not Miranda's father, then equally her real father might have only then discovered that he was.'

Lukeson's mobile rang.

'Danny. . . . *Talk of the devil*,' he mouthed silently to Rochester. 'I'm tied up right now. . . . That is a surprise. When? I see. Well, give me time to see where I stand and I'll get back. Yes, it would be good to talk about times past. Danny Marlaux reckons that now that his light here has dimmed, he'll try his luck in the States,' he told Rochester.

'When is he planning on leaving?'

'A couple of days. A week at the most.'

'He'll be—'

'Out of the country and out of reach,' Lukeson said. 'The question is, is Marlaux jumping ship?'

'If he is, guv, we could all grow old, including Marlaux, before we'd get him back.'

'*If* we got him back. If he's guilty, he could easily slip off into South America and vanish, Helen.'

'Would Marlux tell you he was going, if he was guilty?'

'Perhaps. If he figured that openness about his actions would be taken as a sign of innocence.'

'What're you going to do?'

'Nothing much I can do,' Lukeson said morosely. 'We have nothing with which we could put the halters on him. So if he's guilty, we need to prove it. Fast!'

CHAPTER TWELVE

Katherine Stockton entered the room, obviously preferring to be anywhere else. However, when she saw Clive Bailey her mood changed from one of trepidation to one of gladness. 'Hello, Clive,' she said chirpily.

'Hi, Katherine,' Bailey greeted her.

They were old friends meeting.

Lukeson noted a flash of irritation in Charles Stockton's eyes. Why? he wondered. The chummy nature of Katherine and Clive's reunion? That might mean that it was not irritation Lukeson was seeing, but. . . .

Jealousy?

As arranged, before they'd arrived (wisely now as it turned out), Lukeson let Bailey make the running, reckoning that his rescue of Katherine Stockton would have benefits that would flow from renewing the acquaintance of rescuer and rescued. Cynical. But every possible tool at their disposal had to be used.

'You're looking well, Katherine,' Bailey said.

Lukeson learned that Clive Bailey had the seamless lying skills of an ambassador, because Katherine Stockton looked anything but well. Now a teenager, she still had the haunted look she had had in the media when she had been found. Maybe their visit had brought it all back to her, but Andy Lukeson reckoned that the terror had never gone far away.

'No need to fret, darling,' said Charles Stockton. He hugged his daughter to him, but she was obviously uncomfortable with the intimacy. He drew away petulantly. Lukeson wondered about the relationship between father and daughter. Since Katherine's abduction, her mother had died, which must have been hard for her at a time when she needed someone to lean on. Though his experience of Charles Stockton was only minutes old, he could not envisage him in the role of friend and confidant. Clive Bailey had told him that Stockton was something of an ogre. He had doubted that, but he doubted no longer. 'This whole thing is bloody unfair,' he complained to Lukeson. 'What will raking up the past accomplish?'

'Something forgotten or unmentioned at the time of Katherine's abduction might come to the fore, Mr Stockton,' Lukeson said.

'It's been too long. And best forgotten,' Stockton grumbled.

'I don't mind, Dad.' Stockton shot his daughter a furious look. A difficult man to deal with, Lukeson thought. So much more difficult must it be for Katherine. 'If I can help, I'd like to.'

'Be brief,' Stockton groused to Lukeson.

'Any luck finding Miranda?' Katherine enquired.

'Not yet, Katherine,' Clive Bailey said.

She looked from Bailey to Lukeson, and asked, 'Do you think it might be the same man who abducted me?'

179

'An honest answer, Katherine,' Lukeson said. 'Is that we don't know.'

'But it might be?'

'It's a possibility.'

Charles Stockton picked up a newspaper from the couch he was sitting on and brandished a picture of Samuel Curly on its front page. Almost every newspaper carried the same picture of Curly, being led away following his conviction for the abduction of Katherine Stockton. The accompanying story was about Curly's suicide.

'This is the animal who abducted my daughter. Days out of prison and up to his old tricks. I hope he rots in hell, for every scorching second of eternity.'

'We don't believe that Samuel Curly abducted Miranda Watts, Mr Stockon,' Lukeson said. 'In fact there are now doubts that he abducted Katherine.'

'Rubbish!' Stockton grinned snidely. 'Leaves you lot with a problem, doesn't it. . . .'

'What problem would that be?'

'Dead, Curly can't tell you where he's hidden the Watts girl. He's gone and left that girl rotting somewhere, the way he left Katherine to rot.' He cast Bailey a shrewish look. 'Can't depend on luck again, eh. The second the Watts girl went missing, you should have pulled in Curly and beaten her whereabouts out of him.'

Lukeson decided that Charles Stockton was not a nice man. In fact he displayed all the hallmarks of a malicious bully.

'You don't have to talk to these people,' he told Katherine.

'Dad,' she pleaded. 'If it was me who was missing and Miranda Watts could help, wouldn't you want her to?'

'Too kind-hearted for her own good,' Stockton grunted. 'Just like her mother was. Always someone's fool.'

'How have you been, Katherine?' Lukeson was surprised by Clive Bailey's smooth, honeyed voice (normally more inclined towards an unattractive higher pitch), and his near father confessor demeanour, which was at odds with his usual restless manner. Maybe, Lukeson thought, he and everyone else had underestimated Bailey. He went and sat alongside Katherine. 'Good, I hope?'

'Bad dreams now and then.'

'They'll pass, Katherine,' Bailey said softly, his voice as rich as molten molasses.

'I'm around, thanks to you, Clive,' she mumbled shyly.

Andy Lukeson caught Charles Stockton's look Bailey's way, in which he reckoned there was more than a shade of envy, and thought: Don't overdo the old pals bit. There's a good lad, Clive.

'Now, Katherine,' Bailey said coaxingly. 'I'd like to run through once more the day you were abducted, and thereafter up to when *I* rescued you.' He laid heavy emphasis on the personal, hopefully to make Katherine Stockton beholden.

Her reply confirmed that it had.

'I owe everything to you, Clive,' she said.

Clive Bailey magnanimously waved her statement aside. 'Nonsense. You were a very brave girl, Katherine, whom I was very fortunate to have rescued.'

Charles Stockton's colour was rising higher by the second.

'Can we get on with this?' he barked.

Yes, do get on with it, Lukeson thought. You've milked it

enough. The danger he saw now was Clive Bailey's desire to be in the limelight; a danger that could easily have him overplay his hand and have them both tossed out on their ear. But there was nothing he could do to re-direct Bailey, without risking the derailing of the strategy upon which they had agreed; a strategy that was working much better than he had anticipated.

Lukeson could only hope that the copper in Bailey would overcome the showman.

'What's the point of this?' Charles Stockton challenged Lukeson. 'What happened is all a matter of record. You can see that my daughter is distressed.'

About to attempt pouring oil on troubled waters, Lukeson was upstaged by Bailey, who cajoled: 'If you just run through the sequence of events again, Katherine. Please.'

Flushed, Stockton jumped to his feet. 'That's enough! Old wounds are best left unopened. Please leave now.'

'He had foul breath,' Katherine said quickly. She grimaced. 'I can smell it now. Awful breath. As if he was rotting inside.'

'I don't recall you mentioning that at the time?' Bailey said.

'No, I didn't. Slipped my mind.'

Charles Stockton was again about to interrupt, but Lukeson's look his way stopped him.

Clive Bailey, conscious of Lukeson's supremacy, now that his point about the calming passage of time had proven to be correct was on firmer ground and pressed ahead:

'Go back to the beginning, Katherine, would you, please?'

'If it helps, Clive. I had parted company with my friend Ken Wright. . . .'

Stockton scoffed, making it plain how lowly he rated Wright.

'Dad. Ken is nice. Was nice,' she hastily amended when Stockton glared at her. Which suggested that he had given the thumbs down to any association between Wright and his daughter.

'The whole bloody family are wastrels!'

'That's what you said about Robert Scott as well,' Katherine responded angrily. 'And Ben Smallwood, too.'

Obviously, Katherine having a boyfriend, even a childhood male friend, troubled Charles Stockton no end. A fact that had Andy Lukeson thinking very dark thoughts indeed.

'Go on, Katherine,' Bailey murmured encouragingly.

'I was walking along Cherrytree Lane. A van passed. A couple of minutes later, coming round a sharp corner, I saw the van parked up ahead. I took no notice. It was parked outside a house. It was only later that I got to know that the house was for sale and empty. I suppose it was clever of him that he parked outside the house, to give the idea that he was inside.'

Tears sprang to Katherine Stockton's eyes as the horror of that afternoon rushed back. Composing herself, she went on:

'I went past the van. I hadn't gone far when I was grabbed from behind. I felt what I took to be a knife in my back. He told me not to turn around. If I did he would finish me off. He put tape over my mouth and a hood over my head. He bundled me into the back of the van and drove away. He took me to the caravan. He bound my hands and feet, hands behind my back. He left the hood on me, and the tape on my mouth. Then he left and locked me in.'

'Good girl,' Bailey said, and squeezed Katherine's hand.

Stockton glared at Lukeson, who thought that life could not be very easy living on one's own as Katherine was with such a possessive father.

'You said that his voice sounded funny,' Bailey said.

'Look—'

Lukeson stymied Stockton's protest. 'Shan't be much longer, Mr Stockton.'

Katherine Stockton's brow furrowed. 'Maybe he thought that if he spoke normally I'd recognize his voice, do you think?'

'Did you think that he was serious when he said that he'd finish you off, Katherine?'

She thought about the answer for a long time. Then: 'No, I don't think so.'

'Why?'

'I'm not sure. I was frightened, yes. But I never thought that he'd kill me.'

'Why?' Bailey pressed.

'Just a feeling,' she said vaguely.

'Why did you think he abducted you, Katherine?'

'Why the hell do you think,' Stockton growled. 'Bloody obvious, I'd say.'

'Did you see his hands, Katherine?'

'His hands, Clive?'

'Yes.'

'No. Don't think so. Well, I can't say for sure. It all happened so fast. All a bit of a blur, really.'

'OK. That's perfectly understandable, but think. Were

his hands big or small? Soft, hard?'

Katherine Stockton thought long before she answered. 'Office hands, I'd say. That's the best I can do. Sorry. I was scared stiff.'

'One last question.' Katherine Stockton looked at Andy Lukeson, as if she had forgotten he was present. 'Can you remember the colour of the van?'

'Green,' she said unwaveringly. 'Faded. A bit of a banger.'

'Make?'

'Sorry. Don't know my cars very well.'

'Thank you, Katherine,' Lukeson said. 'Shall we leave it for now?'

'Don't come back,' Charles Stockton said, on seeing them out.

'You said at the time that you could not think of anyone in business or in your personal life that you might have crossed who—'

'Yes I did, Sergeant. And nothing's changed. My daughter was abducted by some bloody pervert, and I don't know any perverts!'

'How can you be sure, Mr Stockton?' Lukeson said. 'How can any of us be sure?'

'That's an uplifting thought,' he barked, before slamming the front door shut.

'He must be one bastard to have to live with,' DC Clive Bailey said.

'Possessive sort would you say, Clive?'

'Obsessive would better describe him, I think.'

'Maybe to the point of wanting his daughter exclusively to himself, would you say?'

'Wouldn't surprise me. What're you getting at?'

'Katherine Stockton said that, though she was

frightened, she never really thought she was in real danger from her abductor. What if there wasn't any danger?'

'You mean that her abduction was a set-up by Stockton to . . . what?'

'Make her dependent on him as her guardian, perhaps? Well?' Lukeson prompted, when Bailey took an age to answer.

'I can see the possibilities,' Bailey said.

'But?'

Again, Bailey thought long and hard before answering. 'The truth?'

'Always.'

'A bit off the wall, I think.' They were walking to their car when, a moment later, Bailey said: 'To put a tape on someone's mouth while struggling, the abductor would have to have had manual dexterity above and beyond, wouldn't you say?'

'I would, Clive.'

'Samuel Curly was an odd job man. His hands would have been big and rough. Katherine described her abductor as having *office hands*. Seems Curly really was shafted.'

'A green van,' Lukeson said. 'Albert Dotty has a green van. A banger?'

'It's certainly seen better days. Faded, too.'

'Wonder if he had it back when Katherine Stockton was abducted?' Lukeson phoned for a check on Dotty's van. 'Dotty's been the owner of the van for the past six years,' was the outcome.

'He didn't own it then when Stockton was abducted. Who was the owner before Dotty?'

'A man by the name of Alistair Burke. He owned the vehicle for three years prior to trading it in.'

'The time frame is right. Local?'

'Brigham.'

'As good as.'

'You did well with Katherine Stockton,' Lukeson complimented.

'Thanks,' Bailey said dully.

'You don't like this end of the business, do you?'

'Hate it.'

'Why did you become a copper, then?'

'I've asked myself that a thousand times.' He chuckled. 'Haven't you?'

'No.'

'You're having me on.'

'Only nine hundred and ninety nine times,' Lukeson said. They laughed together. Andy Lukeson held a hand out to Clive Bailey. 'As soon as this is over, I'll recommend an immediate return to the Training Division.'

'Appreciated, Andy.'

CHAPTER THIRTEEN

'Nice of you to drop by, Andy. Wouldn't blame you if you hadn't after that, ah. . . .' Danny Marlaux grinned the boyish smile that had broken so many female hearts in its day, and still could, Lukeson reckoned, 'shall we say, exchange of views.' Lukeson wondered why, when he could have most women in the palm of his hand, Danny Marlaux had hitched himself to a woman as plain and dumpy as Georgina Adams. She could, of course, be dynamite between the sheets. But Lukeson suspected that she was much too nervy and uptight to be playful. The old adage of never judging a book by its cover came to mind. Marlaux held up the whisky he was holding in invitation to Lukeson to join him.

'Driving, Danny.'

'Just one.'

'A small one.'

'Of course. We can't have an officer of the law over the limit, eh.' Lukeson could not be sure if Marlaux was mocking him. Probably, he decided. 'Like I said, never had you figured as a copper, Andy.'

'And like I said, never had you figured as a bigshot gee-

gee trainer, Danny.'

'Life is a funny old thing, isn't it.'

Marlaux's eyes were mirrors to the past he was reflecting on somewhat sadly, Lukeson thought. He had lost the raw look of the council estate he had been brought up in. The man who had replaced the boy was fashionably jaded looking, and the crinkly hair had been smoothened out and flowed, again fashionably, to collar length with just a suggestion that it might grow longer. The eyes, brown when Andy Lukeson had shared a schooldesk with him, were now blue – contacts. Danny's sight had never been great, but that had stood him well, because his concentrated stare seemed to draw girls in, and later women; women like Sarah Watts and a string of equally high profile and highly sexual women. Hence, Lukeson thought, the jaded look. His hands, too, had lost the redness Lukeson remembered. The hand now holding the whisky he was offering, was soft and well manicured, gone were the stubby fingers and bitten nails of Danny Marlaux's youth.

Marlaux and Lukeson had been good mates as boys and teenagers, but now Lukeson thought that it would be impossible for them to be as close as they had been, if in fact they could be friends at all. Their worlds had diverged to a point that would make friendship impossible, and probably undesirable also.

The double scotch Marlaux had poured for himself lasted all of ten seconds, one in a long line, Lukeson reckoned. Maybe the jaded look was indicative of too much alcohol instead of too much sex. 'How did you end up being a copper?' Just a hint of Marlaux's root accent showed over his now Oxfordish speech. 'Where we came from, being a copper was not a career choice.'

'Well, I followed my old man into the washing machine factory. Six months later, production was moved to Shanghai, just about the time that there was a recruitment drive on for the police.'

'Better than making washing machines, I suppose.'

What a supercilious prat Marlaux had become. He went and topped up his whisky and drank liberally of the refill. While he was drinking, Lukeson took in the elegant country surroundings of what the maid who had answered his knock had described as the drawing room.

'Free tomorrow afternoon?' Marlaux enquired. 'Just a bit of a finger-food bash, I'm afraid.'

'No, I'm not free,' Lukeson said coolly, surprised that, under the circumstances, Marlaux should be holding a social gathering.

'Arranged some time ago, Andy,' he said, reading his thoughts. 'Life goes on, eh.'

'For some,' Lukeson said, cooler still.

'If you think I'm a bastard, say so.' Marlaux's speech now had no definite regional bias, just the universal slurredness of a drunk.

'You're a bastard, Danny!'

For a moment, before he dropped on to a chair, spent, Lukeson had readied himself to parry Marlaux's expected lunge. He asked bitterly:

'How is that bitch I married.'

'Worried.'

Marlaux laughed drunkenly. 'Sarah worries about Sarah, end of!'

'A bit harsh, wouldn't you say?' Lukeson said.

'No, I wouldn't,' Danny Marlaux stated emphatically.

'Only one thing mattered to Sarah, her bloody career. She hated Miranda from the instant she was a first cell in her womb. And that hatred grew. Oh, she was careful to foster her public image of a loving parent. But when the crowd left and the cameras stopped flashing, she quickly relegated Miranda and yours truly to the wings, while she got on with her busy life.'

The second person to cast doubt on the quality and nature of Sarah Watts relationship with her daughter, given by her former husband, who would have had up-close experience of that relationship. Sarah Watts was getting a lot of bad press.

Warranted? Or simply Marlaux's griping?

'Sarah's self-interest and self-promotion left no room for family, Andy.'

Lukeson had never seen Danny Marlaux weep, but he came close to seeing tears now.

'Do you think your former wife is involved in your daughter's disappearance, Danny?' Lukeson asked quietly.

Marlaux looked aghast. 'God, no. True. She's a cold-hearted bitch. But she'd never harm Miranda.'

'And you?'

'Me?'

'You,' Lukeson confirmed.

Danny Marlaux's face set in stone. 'Now who's being a bastard.'

'You didn't answer my question, Danny?'

'Neither one of us would stoop to harming our daughter.'

'Miranda is not your daughter.'

'I think of her as such.'

'Then why did you walk out on her?'

'Not on her. On her mother.'

'Miranda was just a kid. Hard for her to distinguish, wouldn't you say.'

'I explained.'

'No point, Danny. If the subject matter is beyond understanding. I'll be blunt. . . .'

'What have you been?'

'Both you and your former wife are in a financial bind. The insurance policy on Miranda in the event of her being kidnapped would help you both out of the proverbial.'

'You prick!' Marlaux lunged at Lukeson. His punch toppled Lukeson backwards over an ocassional table. He attempted to follow through, but the whisky sloshing about in his legs had him staggering sideways to fall alongside Lukeson on the floor. 'Fuck off out of my sight, Andy,' he growled. 'And never come back.' This time his accent was unmistakeably the accent of his birth.

Lukeson stood up and helped Marlaux to his feet.

'Can't guarantee I won't be back, Danny,' he said. 'But not as a friend. What was Simon Bennett's relationship with Miranda?'

'I wasn't around when Bennett was shagging Sarah.' He held Lukeson's gaze. '*Relationship?*'

Lukeson told Marlaux about the photographs they had found in Bennett's room. Incensed, he smashed the whisky glass he was holding against the far wall of the room. 'I'll rip the bastard's heart out!' Lukeson now saw in Danny Marlaux's brashness and jadedness the demons of rejection and loneliness. His initial envy of what appeared to be Marlaux's life of privilege vanished. He would not swap with him for one moment. In fact he had never before felt as sorry for any man. Marlaux was adrift in a sea of lonliness. He ruled Marlaux out as a suspect, and hoped he hadn't called it wrong. Moved to pity, he said:

'What would you say to a good old-fashioned pint, in a good old-fashioned pub, Danny. The kind we knew.'

'I'd like that, Andy,' Danny Marlaux said, with genuine warmth.

'Well, let's find one right now.'

'We can take a trip down memory lane,' Marlaux said enthusiastically. Then, wearily: 'You don't know how often I've gone back there, to the narrow streets and alleyways, when the horseshit, if you'll pardon the pun, got too much for me.'

'A penny for them.' DC Charlie Johnson looked up from the canteen cod and chips he'd been staring at, miles away. 'Mind if I...?' Taking it for granted that Johnson would not refuse her company, Anne Fenning pulled out a chair and sat down. 'If you don't mind my saying so, Charlie. You look bothered.'

'That's because I am bothered.'

'What about?'

'If I knew that then I wouldn't be bothered, would I?' he responded sharply. Fenning went to leave. 'Oh, sit down you silly cow.' Frustrated, Johnson said, 'There's something niggling at the back of my mind, Anne . . . just beyond my reach. It's driving me crazy.'

'Something to do with Miranda Watts's abduction?'

'Yes. Something I heard. Something I saw, maybe. I don't know. But it's in there,' he tapped his forehead, 'locked away, and I haven't got the combination to release it.'

'Sometimes, I find that if I put it out of mind, it pops to

mind. If you get my meaning.' Johnson pushed the sodden cod and chips away from him. 'That's an awful waste of good food,' Fenning rebuked him.

'Good food,' he snorted. 'Here! Wash out your mouth, WPC Fenning! If a rumour like that were to get around, it would destroy this canteen's reputation.'

At that moment, DC Helen Rochester was ringing the doorbell of Alistair Burke's front door in Brigham. 'Alistair Burke?' she enquired of the man who answered her summons. The man's eyes fixed on the Brigham PC who had accompanied Rochester, made to dash past them, changed his mind and slammed the door shut.

'You again!' It pleased PC Brian Scuttle that his presence, and that of two other uniforms on her doorstep, upset Sylvia Planter. On cue, Arthur appeared in the hallway behind her. 'What now?'

'We've come to have a look round,' Scuttle said, brandishing a search warrant. 'This is a—'

'I know what it is,' Planter said.

'Then you'll know that it allows us to enter and search unhindered.'

The caution was for Arthur, Planter's minder, who seemed caught between bold action and retreat. Scuttle knew well that men like Arthur, undecided between courses of action, often chose the wrong one.

'Leave it be, Arthur,' Planter said, sensing his crossroads dilemma. 'You lot think I've done for Miranda Watts, don't you. I might have got up to a few things I'm not proud of in me time, but I'd never harm a child.'

Scuttle moved forward. Planter stepped aside.

'Get on with it then. Do what you've come to do. Then clear off. Nazi bastards,' she called after the search team when they entered the house. 'You'll find nothing.'

'Round back!' Helen Rochester ordered the young Brigham PC, who seemed rooted to the spot by what had happened.

Andy Lukeson placed a pint of bitter on the pub table in front of Danny Marlaux and sat opposite him, letting Marlaux choose his own time to return from wherever his memories had taken him. He eventually picked up the pint of bitter, sipped, and said, 'You know, sometimes, more often than you think, I've wished to be back in the old neighbourhood, Andy. Maybe even be kids again. Have old Potter laying into us for not trying hard enough.' His laughter was moodily reflective. 'Or for not trying at all. I hated homework. Only one thing I hated more and that was Potter.' He grimaced. 'And that goo that was always at the corners of his mouth.'

Lukeson said, 'With powers of observation like yours you should have been a copper too.'

'You never married, Andy.'

'Never met the right woman, I suppose. A couple of close calls though.'

'Anyone right now?'

Lukeson shook his head, wishing that he could have said Sally Speckle.

Danny Marlaux slumped in his chair, seeming at least a foot shorter, and an age older. 'Wish I hadn't. Married, I mean. . . .'

'Because it doesn't always work out, doesn't mean it's

not worth trying, Danny.'

Locked into his own world, Marlaux wasn't listening.

'I might have never known. . . .'

'Known what?'

'Remember all those birds I pulled. . . .'

'How could I forget, always playing catch up as I was. With never a hope of matching your head count.'

'I could never figure it out, you know, Andy.'

'Figure what out?'

'How I didn't have an army of brats.' It was something which Lukeson had often wondered about also. He had assumed that it was all down to good planning. But good planning had been at odds with Danny Marlaux's tomcat nature. 'Didn't you ever think about it, Andy? You must have.'

'It came to mind a time or two,' he admitted honestly.

'I thought, having an Irish gran, I'd got a rub of the green. When I heard a voice on the phone telling me that Miranda was not mine, it hit me like the proverbial ton of bricks. I went along and had the test done.' By the pain in Danny Marlaux's face, Lukeson knew what was coming. 'I've been firing blanks, Andy.'

Not knowing what to say, Lukeson said nothing at all.

DC Helen Rochester thought about vaulting – American cop style – the side gate in pursuit of the man she assumed was Alistair Burke, but thought better of it, and simply opened it. The man had not waited around to confirm his name, so it was a reasonable assumption to make that he was Alistair Burke. And how significant was it that he had taken to his heels. Maybe theirs was a call which Alistair Burke had been expecting for a long time – in fact, since Katherine Stockton's abduction.

For a man whom Rochester put in late sixties, Burke had a turn of speed that belied his age. Clearly his intention was to reach a garden gate to make his escape through. It was a valiant try, but Burke was no match for the young PC, Rochester reckoned. She could only count her blessings that Brigham had insisted on her being accompanied on their patch. Had she been on her own, Burke would be long gone.

She held her breath when it seemed that the PC would bring Burke down in a rugby tackle, thinking about the inevitable lurid stories about broken bones and police brutality. However, the young constable opted for getting ahead to block the garden gate, bringing to an end Burke's dash for freedom.

'Do be sensible, Mr Burke,' Rochester said, when it seemed he was going to charge the PC.

The grit left Burke, like air escaping a balloon. He surrendered quietly. Defeated, he told Rochester, 'I should never have done it. I knew that sooner or later you'd get round to me and find out the awful thing I did.'

'What awful thing shouldn't you have done, Mr Burke?' Helen Rochester enquired quietly.

'When Sarah Watts, catwalk queen, agreed to hitch herself to me, I admit I was chuffed senseless, Andy. . . .'

'You had every right to be chuffed, Danny,' Lukeson said. 'A trainer on the up. And now a wife that raised men's blood pressure to dangerous levels.'

'Yeah. Danny Marlaux had made good. But I hadn't, Andy. It was all smoke and mirrors. Deep inside, I was still Danny Marlaux, working class boy. The longer I lived with Sarah, and moved in her ritzy circle of friends, the more I came to realize that she kept me around as her. . . .' He groaned. 'Work of charity. A kind of trophy. Look at me. The chic, classy Sarah Watts, being kind to the poor boy made good. But made good by her. I began to understand that my success as a trainer was down to her influencing friends to stable their horses with me. It pissed me off, Andy. But, surprisingly, I wasn't rash enough to pitch it all to blazes. Then the horses which had been placed with me as favours to Sarah began to win, and lo-and-behold Danny Marlaux was having horses stabled with him because Danny Marlaux was a damn good trainer.

'Then one day, a bombshell. . . .

'Told you,' said Sylvia Planter triumphantly to Scuttle when the search team was leaving empty handed. 'But, nuisance that you lot are, I still hope that you'll find Miranda Watts safe and sound.'

Unsure about how to interpret Planter's sentiment, Brian Scuttle declared, with a confidence he was far from feeling: 'We will. And we'll also find who took her,' he added, holding the medium's gaze, searching her face for a hint of guilt or apprehension, but seeing none. But then she had to be a very good actress to make people believe that she could contact the other world.

'If you like, I could ask my Inspector Armitage to—'

'Give over,' Scuttle scoffed.

'I knew about your former girlfriend having passed over,' she reminded Scuttle.

'A shot in the dark.'

'Sparklers.' Walking off, Scuttle spun around. 'Your secret nickname for her. If you change your mind about my offer of help, drop by.' Sylvia Planter closed the front door of the cottage.

Rooted to the spot as if struck by lightning, one of the search team asked a shaken Scuttle, 'What was that all about?'

'I wish I knew,' said Brian Scuttle, very quietly.

'Cheated, of course,' said Burke, in reply to Helen Rochester's question about the awful thing he'd done.

'Cheated?'

'Didn't really mean to. But once I'd started, it was all too easy. Besides, I needed the money. This old ramshackle of a house eats up money. Always something or other needing doing.'

'You've lost me, Mr Burke,' Rochester said.

'Lost you? You can't have forgotten why you came. Will they put me away for a long time, do you think?'

'Depends,' Rochester hedged.

'On what?'

'On how serious this something is that you've done.'

'It was easy,' he said reflectively. 'So very easy. I suppose I'd better start at the beginning.'

'Yes. That would be best.'

'First, would you mind moving a little. You're standing right on top of him, you see. There was a flowerbed there,' he went on matter-of-factly. 'I hated to have to . . . but it was the easiest spot to dig. . . .'

'Mr Burke.' He looked curiously at Rochester. 'Are you telling me that there's someone buried here?'

'Bombshell?'

Danny Marlaux laughed drunkenly and loudly, the beer

catching up with the copious whiskies from earlier, earning the curious annoyance of fellow imbibers and, more importantly, the landlord. Marlaux beckoned to Lukeson to come closer. 'The Goddess wasn't what she seemed, Andy,' he confided in a schoolboy confidence, accompanied by a schoolboy giggle. 'All that swank.' Now he was suddenly bitter. 'While all the time she was muck, just like me! Even more mucky than me.'

Lukeson recalled that Sarah Watts's publicity had her as the offspring of a train driver and an advertising executive.

'All bollocks, Andy. A foggy station platform. Two people from the opposite ends of the social ladder meet. Fall in love at first sight.' He laughed mockingly. 'A whiff of romance is a whole lot better than the grimness of being adopted when her old man, blind drunk, was run down by a bus after her mother had died from a drug overdose a month earlier,' he roared angrily, his hand sweeping across the table to knock over the beer, splashing a nearby woman.

'OK!' The landlord came from behind the bar. 'Out. Now! Any messing and I'll call the police,' he informed Lukeson.

'Come on, Danny.' Lukeson grabbed Marlaux by the arm. Marlaux fought back, but Lukeson brought his restraint skills to bear. Having had on many ocassions called for help, the landlord was quick to spot a copper at work. 'I'll need a taxi. If you'd oblige.'

'Yeah. Sure.'

'I'll wait outside.'

'Appreciated,' the landlord said. 'There's a cab company a couple of streets away, I'll give them a bell. Shouldn't be long.'

'Thanks.'

'Yes,' Burke replied in answer to Rochester's question.

'Who?' was the obvious question.

'My brother Alistair.'

'I thought you were Alis—'

'Heaven forbid. I'd hate to be called Alistair. Can't stand the name. No, I'm Alfred, Alistair's older brother, but only by two years. Not much, is it.'

'Tell me what happened, Mr Burke.'

'We had an argument, Alistair and me. We argued a lot. Prickly, that was Alistair. Always demanding his own way. I wanted to watch a programme about the Tudors. Alistair hated history. I loved history. Alastair loved quiz shows. I hate quiz shows. Went at it hammer and thongs. And just when I won, I rarely won, Alistair went all pucy looking and dropped dead. I thought, of course, about phoning the police. I knew it was too late for a doctor or an ambulance. But then the police might think that I'd caused his death. I suppose in a way I did, didn't I. So I buried him.'

Alfred Burke's face became a mask of misery.

'Then, that night, I had the most dreadful dream. I dreamed that Alistair had only fainted. That I'd buried him alive. But it was too late,' he said philosophically, 'So I let him be. When Friday came round, there it was, on the bedside locker where he always left it. Alistair's pension book. The name on it was A. Burke. A for Alistair. A for Alfred. It was fate. So I went and drew Alistair's pension. Such a terrible thing to do. I was quite, quite ashamed of myself.'

Mad as a hatter, thought Rochester. It seemed that in his mind fiddling the welfare, and not having possibly buried his brother alive was his cardinal sin. But the purpose of her visit was still a live issue. Though dead, Alistair Burke could still have been Katherine Stockton's abductor.

DC Charlie Johnson yelped and swore profusely when, leaving the canteen, still preoccupied he cracked his shin against the edge of the door.

'Oooh. That's painful,' Anne Fenning sympathized.

'Why can't I just get hold of what's bothering me,' he complained.

'Like I told you. The more you try, the less you'll get. Let it be, and whatever it is will pop into your head when you least expect it to.'

'I'll be in touch, Danny,' Lukeson promised, resisting Marlaux's attempt to pull him into the taxi. He gave the driver Marlaux's address and the fare.

'Settle down, mate,' the cab driver barked, when again Marlaux tried to pull Lukeson into the cab as it moved off. 'I'm not at all sure I want this fare.' Lukeson recognized a ploy for a sweetener. He handed over a tenner, and didn't bother to argue. 'Well, he'll probably pass out any minute, so I'll risk it.'

'I thought you might,' Lukeson mumbled, as the cab drove off.

He was of a mind to go home, but instead decided to return to the station – to do what, he wasn't sure. Hope, probably, that something in some report would catch his eye and make sense of the seemingly disparate bits and pieces.

*

'What did Alistair do for a living, Mr Burke?' Rochester enquired.

'A living?' Alfred Burke laughed as if he'd heard the joke of all jokes. 'Oh, how he'd have hated that. A living! Alistair fancied himself as a concert pianist, which he wasn't,' he said spitefully. 'Took really good care of his hands. Poofy. That was Alistair. Used up a bloody ocean of handcream to keep his hands soft and agile. "Must keep my manual dexterity." ' Alfred Burke's impersonation of his brother was decidedly camp. ' "You'll see, Alfred," ' he'd say. ' "My big break will come." There was no telling him that a scholarship of six months learning the classical piano would never make him a concert pianist.'

Bet you often reminded him of that, Rochester thought.

'He played the weekends in bars and clubs.' Again he mimicked his late brother. ' "It's only until my public will recognize my genius, Alfred." A bloody ivory tinkler, that's all he was. Work shy, was Alistair. Worked for all of six months in his life. It wasn't much of a job for a genius. Even had to have his own transport. A company executive, was how he described himself. Hah! A bit much for someone selling adhesive tape door-to-door, don't you think.'

'Did Alistair ever visit Loston in his capacity as a salesman?'

'Must have. It's not far away, is it. It was a here-there-everywhere kind of job.'

'When did your brother do this job?'

'Oh, a long time ago.'

'How long would long be, Alfred?'

'Eight. Maybe nine years ago.'

Around the time Katherine Stockton had been abducted.

'Can't be sure. He was too bloody old to be traipsing around door-to-door anyway.'

Just when she was considering Alistair Burke as Katherine Stockton's abductor, Rochester's victory was snatched away.

'Cruel blow,' said Alfred Burke guiltily. 'Money was short. It always was.' Burke's excuse for what was to come. 'I pushed Alistair in to painting the exterior of the house. He came crashing off the ladder. Shattered his right wrist. The bone cracked like a dropped china teacup, and in as many pieces too. It was pretty useless for anything after that.'

Not the kind of hand that would be much use in an abduction, Rochester thought.

'Couldn't play the piano anymore. That's why he took that awful salesman's job. All my fault,' he said miserably.

'If you'll go along with the constable now, Mr Burke,' Rochester said wearily.

'Will I go to gaol for defrauding the Social?' Alfred Burke was suddenly a frail, frightened, elderly man.

'I don't expect you'll be going to gaol, Mr Burke,' Rochester said truthfully.

Alfred Burke's detention would, of course, be in a prison of sorts. One possibly even more terrifying than the norm.

Lukeson looked grimly at the desk phone (he'd powered off his mobile), none too pleased at the interruption. However, his annoyance vanished on hearing Sally Speckle. 'Burning the midnight oil, eh, Andy,' she said. A lousy day had suddenly got better.

'You know how it is. Paperwork to be completed. Reports to be gone through.'

'Any progress in finding Miranda Watts?'

'A couple of promising lines of inquiry.'

'Copperspeak for standstill.'

'If you were here, you'd likely have the mess sorted out by now, Sally.' It was Lukeson's round about way of asking when or *if* she would be back.

'I'm not sure the red carpet would be out for me if I returned, Andy.' He had never heard her feel so insecure.

'Dont be daft. The door is open. All you have to do is walk through.'

There ensued a long contemplative silence, before she spoke again. 'The thing is, Andy. I'm not sure I want to be a copper anymore.'

'New interests?'

Meaning, new boyfriend?

'Now that I've had time to think about it, I'm not sure I ever really wanted to be a copper. Of course I can't remain here forever, doing nothing.' That was good news. 'Although West Cork is a little bit of heaven that fell to earth, peaceful and restful, jobs hereabouts are as scarce as snowflakes in a heatwave. But I don't want to go back to being a copper, simply because I can't find anything else to do.'

The man's voice, the same voice he'd heard before, was a dagger to Andy Lukeson's heart. An image of a man at ease came to mind.

'What do you think, Andy?'

'Not for me to say.' He sounded terse and disinterested. 'But you could give it one more try, I suppose.' Worse. He had tried to redeem himself, and had only sounded condescending and even more disinterested. Bloody hell, he thought. Tell her out straight that you ... what? He missed her, yes. But how deep did his feelings go. He couldn't be sure without testing them, and up to now he hadn't had the bottle to do so, gripped as he was and had been by a fear of having a copious amount of egg on his face. And, of course, had he tried to begin a relationship, win or lose, the personal would change the professional. In his time he had seen too many in-house relationships end in tears.

'Being a copper is not something you do just for a living, is it,' Speckle said matter-of-factly, seemingly unaware of his confusion. Or uncaring, perhaps? 'At least not in my book. And I suspect not in yours either, Andy. Appalling hours. No social life. Time off is a lottery. And canteen food that defies digestion. Being a copper is more a vocation than a job, isn't it.'

Lukeson wanted to give whole-hearted encouragement to Sally Speckle to return to work, but he did not want to push her into something that she was obviously undecided about and might not want at all having returned. When it came down to it they could talk all day and all night, but in the end she would have to make up her own mind.

'Be a darling and put some more coal on the fire.'

Lukeson heard the man, Fergal, he supposed, groan: 'Must I?'

'Go on. It's chilly.'

Another groan. Lukeson could imagine him rising reluctantly, very reluctantly, from being stretched out, his head in Sally's lap. Red hair, green eyes and ruddy complexion, was the picture that presented itself to Lukeson, unfairly so. But hatred and jealousy were powerful distorting forces.

'I've got to go.'

'Of course,' Speckle said. Not unduly perturbed, it would seem. 'Phone soon, Andy.'

He hung up, resisting the urge to slam the phone down. He had been weary when he'd loaded Danny Marlaux into a cab, but now, suddenly, his weariness had become bone tiredness. His mood (despite having had a commendable coup in Elk) was low. He was beginning to feel the heavy hand of failure with regard to Miranda Watts. Perhaps Sarah Watts's appeal on the morrow would bring results. But with mass coverage in the media without response, he would not hold his breath.

On reaching the station carpark, Helen Rochester was arriving back from her trip to Brigham. 'All very interesting,' he responded glumly when she brought him up to speed on Alfred Burke and his misdeeds. 'But we're no nearer finding Katherine Stockton's abductor, who may also be Miranda Watts's.' He was getting into his car when he realized how priggishly off-hand he had been. 'Oh, Helen. . . .' She paused, turned, disappointment still on her face. 'Sorry. Well done.'

'You have a lot on your mind, guv,' she said graciously. ' 'Night.'

'I've got it!'

'Good for you,' said the woman in bed with DC Charlie Johnson, deadpan. 'I was beginning to check for a pulse.'

'Sorry. Something's been niggling at me.'

'I know the feeling.'

'Mucky trainers!'

'What?'

'Mucky trainers,' Johnson repeated. 'She was wearing

207

mucky trainers!'

'You want *me* to wear mucky trainers. Is that what you're saying?' The woman was shaking her head vehemently. 'I'm a straightforward old-fashioned girl.'

'It might be nothing at all,' he enthused.

'You'd say, would you,' the woman said sceptically, warily slipping out of bed.

'But mucky trainers might make all the difference!'

The woman watched bewildered as Johnson leaped out of bed and picked up the bedside phone. She had never seen a man starkers using the phone before, but now that she had, she found it decidedly off-putting. She could only wonder if mucky trainers would make a difference. She decided that she was not going to wait around to find out.

'Where are you going?' Johnson asked, not really interested in her reply.

'Some place safe.'

'Andy. Mucky trainers.'

Andy. What had she got herself into, the woman pondered, gathering her clothes and dressing quickly. Closing the door of the flat, she glanced back and thought that Charlie Johnson had a well shaped bum. She might have changed her mind, before Charlie said:

'The grave. I think I might know who dug it.'

All hope of sleep gone, Lukeson let his mind sift through reports and interviews, going over and over old ground again and again until his thoughts came together in a flash of insight. It might be 4.30 in the morning, but that was not going to stop him phoning Danny Marlaux. He was not pleased. The previous night's bender had taken its inevitable toll. 'Won't keep you from your sleep for long,

Danny. You told me last night that Sarah Watts's early life was not all it was cracked up to be.'

'So?' Marlaux said peevishly.

'Is Sarah Watts your former wife's real name, Danny?'

'I suppose.'

'You don't know?' Lukeson asked increduously. 'Who would know?'

'What's this all about?'

'Who would know, Danny?' Lukeson insisted.

'Jimmy Mullins, I reckon.'

'Who's he?'

'Sarah's former manager and PR guru. She always said that he made her from nothing.'

'Where would I find him?'

'At this hour, probably shagging one of his models. What's this all about?' Marlaux asked again, and was again ignored by Lukeson.

'Have you by any chance got Mullins's telephone number or address?'

'Not my type.'

'Cut out the arsing around, Danny! This is important.'

'Why not ask Sarah what her real name is, if Watts isn't? OK. OK,' Marlaux groaned when Lukeson was about to launch into a tirade. 'His number might be in an old diary I've got. If I've still got it. And if I can find it, if I've got it.'

'Give me patience,' Lukeson grunted.

Lukeson drummed out a tattoo with his fingers on the bedside locker anxiously awaiting Marlaux's return.

'Still there?' Marlaux said, ten minutes later.

'Did you find the diary?'

'Yeah.'

'On the moon, was it.'

'You can be a cantankerous bastard, can't you.'

'Have you got Mullins's number?'

He reeled off the telephone number. 'Of course that's from a long time ago. It might be changed by now.'

'Not a problem.'

'Nothing is for coppers,' Marlaux said sourly.

'Thanks, Danny. Sorry for disturbing you.'

'In a pig's eye you are!'

The phone went dead.

It seemed that Danny Marlaux knew Mullins well. 'I'd like to speak to Mr Mullins,' Lukeson informed the breathless woman who answered the phone.

'Now?' she wailed.

'Right now.'

'Well, you can't. Mr Mullins is busy right now.'

'Police.'

'Police?' she repeated.

'Mr Mullins. Now!'

'Police, Jimmy,' she said.

'At five o'clock in the morning,' Mullins said. 'It's someone takin' the piss!'

'I don't think so, Jimmy.'

'Give me the phone,' he griped. 'Who is this?'

'As the lady said, police,' Lukeson said. 'DS Lukeson, Loston CID to be precise.'

'What d'ya want?' Mullins asked, bemused.

'Sarah Watts's real name.'

'Sarah's real name?' he checked suspiciously.

'Tell you what,' Lukeson said. 'I'll give you the phone number of Loston police. You can phone and check me out.'

'Don't want the bother, do I,' Mullins growled. 'Sarah ain't in my stable no more. Tompkins. Sarah Tompkins.' What had, up to that point, been a ghost of an idea, suddenly took on substance. 'Can I get back to the business in hand, now?'

'Enjoy,' Lukeson said.

He phoned Johnson back, told him what Sarah Watts's real name was.

'Sisters?' Johnson said. 'Linda and Sarah Tompkins.'

'Be a bit of a coincidence if they weren't,' Lukeson said.

'OK. Sisters, Andy. But why would Linda Tompkins abduct her sister's daughter?'

'I reckon I know why, Charlie. . . .'

'Go on, then.'

'It's to do with the book about Sarah Watts which Linda was planning to write. I think that, while researching the book, Linda unearthed Sarah Watts's relationship to her. Now according to Danny Marlaux, Sarah carefully avoided all mention of her less than shining childhood, buying in instead to the PR fiction which Mullins had created as Sarah's background, the offspring of a train driver and an advertizing executive, pure romance for the punters. Then along comes Linda Tompkins threatening to drag Sarah screaming back to reality. Sarah was about to be revealed as a fraud, a mountain of dirty washing in prospect, devastating. Her reaction was to kick Linda out, and want nothing further to do with her. Probably had the whole thing tied up legally. Embittered, Linda Tompkins gets back at her sister by abducting her daughter.'

'You reckon?' Johnson asked, obviously not wholly convinced by Lukeson.

'Only one way to be sure, Charlie. And that's to put it to

Linda Tompkins.'

'Imagine,' Johnson mused. 'It all came down to mucky trainers. And what they might mean on a day when that weird grave was found.'

'You can take a bow, Charlie.'

DC Charlie Johnson chuckled.

'If you're right, Andy, we can both bow until our chins touch the floor!'

CHAPTER FOURTEEN

When Andy Lukeson and Charlie Johnson arrived at Brate Hall, it was shrouded in November mist which gave it a menacing humped-back appearance. 'Dracula would feel at home here,' Johnson said, arriving in the gravelled forecourt. 'Must have at least a dozen ghosts about the place rattling their chains, I reckon.'

A man appeared out of the mist alongside Johnson, causing him to leap back when he spoke: 'What is it you want?'

'Don't creep!' Johnson exploded.

'You didn't answer my question,' the man barked.

'Police,' Lukeson said. 'Is Ms Tompkins about?'

'Kid stayed overnight with Miss Hosford, as he often does.' There was a note of criticism in his voice, Lukeson guessed for Linda Tompkin's off-loading of her child. The man was of an age when parent and child were seldom apart. 'Haven't seen her.'

'Maybe someone else has.'

'She'll be still at home, I reckon.'

'She isn't.'

The man shrugged. 'Ain't her keeper, am I.'

Business done, as far as he was concerned, the man turned and walked away.

'Your name is?' Lukeson asked.

'O'Malley. Michael Francis O'Malley, that would be.'

Irish.

Nationality confirmed, Lukeson had a reason for the man's unfriendliness. Probably quite a hospitable and amiable fellow, if you were not a British copper.

'My colleague and I would appreciate you informing Miss Hosford of our arrival.'

'If it's Miss Hosford you'll be wanting, then come back about midday. Ain't given to early risin', is Letty Hosford.'

'Our business here is urgent,' Lukeson said. 'So be a good fellow and wake her up.'

'Wake her up?' O'Malley chuckled, as if Lukeson's suggestion was pure lunacy. 'She'd skin me alive.'

Ire up, Lukeson lost patience with the Irishman's obstinacy. He was about to read the riot act to him when, behind him, at the corner of the house, he saw the merest movement in the mist. Instinctively, he called out:

'Ms Tompkins?'

The ghostly form ducked out of sight. Almost immediately a motor engine started up. A ramshackle van sped from behind the house and headed straight for them. Johnson bravely stepped into the van's path, but O'Malley grabbed him and pulled him aside. Both men fell in a tangle to the ground. 'The mad bitch was never goin' to stop!' O'Malley told an enraged Johnson, before he realized the truth of what the Irishman had said and thanked him.

Lukeson was already in the car. Johnson scrambled in as he gave pursuit. The twisting nature of the drive on

214

their way up to the house was a challenge. Going in the other direction at high speed was even a greater challenge, and the autumnal muck did not help, needing Lukeson to constantly correct the car's progress to avoid plunging off the drive into the dense undegrowth or, worse still, smacking headlong into a stout English oak. Up ahead the back of the van swayed dangerously. 'She'll kill her bloody self,' Johnson predicted. No sooner had he spoken than the van went into a slide, swerved, and spun across the drive to clip branches as it sped past, then swerved again to the opposite side, corrected itself for a split-second before smashing into a tree. Thick black smoke showed from under the bonnet.

Lukeson was out of the car and running.

'It'll blow, Andy,' Johnson cautioned.

'If she has a breath left in her, I want her to use it to tell me where Miranda Watts is, Charlie.'

Linda Tompkins was sitting very erect. At first, Lukeson marvelled at how she had escaped serious injury, until he saw the spike of shattered steering wheel in her abdomen. Lukeson tried the driver's door but it was jammed fast.

'Try the passenger door,' he ordered Johnson.

'Don't waste your time,' Tompkins said through the open driver's window, her breathing ropey. 'I know when I'm done for. How did you find out?'

'First. Where's Miranda Watts?'

'There's an old disused church on the estate . . . Miranda is in a hideaway.

'Is she alive?'

'Scratches and bruises.' Andy Lukeson's relief was immense. She coughed. Blood seeped between her pursed

215

lips. 'Tell him not to bother,' Linda Tompkins told Lukeson, referring to Johnson summoning an ambulance. 'Even if I could live, I'd not want to live in prison.

'You didn't answer my question. How did you find out?'

'Mucky trainers,' Lukeson said. 'The day when that fake grave was found in the wood near the Watts house, DC Johnson interviewed you. He happened to notice your dirty trainers, and later related them to the sodden wood in which the grave was found. Then when a man called Jimmy Mullins, Sarah Watts's former manager, told me that Sarah Watts real name was Sarah Tompkins, it all fell into place. I reckoned that while researching the book about Sarah you found out that you and Sarah were actually sisters. . . .'

'Clever bastard, aren't you. Came as a hell of a shock, me and Sarah being sisters. We were separated as kids when we were adopted. When I told her what I thought were joyous tidings, she told me to get stuffed. To clear off and not bother her or Miranda ever again. And to keep my brat away from her daughter. She said that she wanted nothing to do with us. She couldn't take the family skeleton returning out of the blue to threaten the lady of the manor.'

Linda Tompkins laughed weakly.

'She really did believe all that publicity rubbish that Mullins had dreamed up. Daft bitch!'

'Being given the heave-ho must have made you angry.'

'That's putting it mildly, Sergeant. The snotty lot she was in with wouldn't half shun her if they knew that she was just a waif from a council estate whose father had been a hopeless drunk, and her mother a druggie. Her world would have crashed down around her.'

216

'You could have still unmasked her. Why didn't you?'

'Oh, I fully intended to. But then, still flaming mad, I found myself in Cherrytree Lane. I stopped to offer Miranda a lift home. She told me that we weren't friends anymore, and to go away. In a rage, the kind I'd never known before, I pulled her into the van to give her a good talking to. When Miranda said that she'd tell her mum about what had happened, that I'd go to jail, and Darren would be left alone, I panicked and kept her with me. Not really knowing how I'd get out of the mess I'd dropped myself in, I needed time to think. But it was already too late.'

Linda Tompkins's breath rattled in her throat.

'I'm glad you came,' she said. 'You see, I was beginning to wonder how I'd get out of the fix I'd got myself into. And there seemed only one way. At least now I won't have to answer for murder.'

'Why the grave?' Lukeson enquired.

'A silly attempt to complicate and confuse.' She grabbed Lukeson's arm. 'Ask Letty to care for Darren. She likes him.' Linda Tompkins smiled weakly, and stopped breathing.

'Andy!' Johnson shouted, and pointed to the sheath of flame engulfing the front of the van. They ran, diving into the undergrowth as it exploded. When they looked up, Letty Hosford was standing some way off, a protective arm around a little boy's shoulders – Darren Tompkins, Lukeson guessed.

'Where's Lukeson?' CS Frank 'Sermon' Doyle demanded to know of DC Helen Rochester for the third time in as many minutes.

'I'm sure he'll be along presently, sir,' she replied, unconvincingly. All she knew was what everyone else knew, and that was that her guv'nor and Charlie Johnson had gone haring off to parts unknown, leaving everyone else to carry the can, which she considered to be bloody inconsiderate.

'Running a bit over time, aren't we, Superintendent,' said a reporter from the Loston Echo. 'Almost twenty minutes in fact.'

Doyle forced his facial muscles into a parody of a smile. 'DS Lukeson had urgent business to attend to. I'm sure—'

'More urgent than finding a missing child?' the same reporter asked, intent on points scoring.

Doyle ignored him and addressed the media gathering in general. 'You'll understand that police inquiries don't always run to schedule. I'm sure that DS Lukeson's explanation, when he arrives, will be satisfactory.'

A cynical murmur rippled through the gathering.

'I'll roast the bastard on an open spit when I get my hands on him,' Doyle told Rochester in a tight-lipped aside.

'Can we get on with this, Chief Superintendent,' Sarah Watts demanded.

'DS Lukeson—'

'Has jumped ship, it seems.'

The assembled media sat up. Nothing like a good old fashioned dust-up to get the adrenalin pumping.

'DS Lukeson is an extremely able and reliable officer,' Doyle said, as calmly as his seething anger with Andy Lukeson would allow him to. 'I'm sure that when he arrives, he'll have a perfectly good reason for not being present.'

'Perhaps, he's searching my home again, Chief Superintendent,' Watts said sarcastically.

The media were now as primed as Olympian sprinters on the starting line.

Irked by what she saw as Watts having a go, Helen Rochester said, 'And maybe, Ms Watts, DS Lukeson has got a lead which he felt it necessary to follow up on. You wouldn't want him to do anything less, would you?'

For Sarah Watts, it was an unanswerable question.

Chewing iron, Doyle said, 'Lukeson's gone too far this time.' He was at a loss to understand, and resented Rochester's lack of interest in what he had said, her focus and attention being behind him.

Good one, Andy, she thought. Hollywood couldn't have done better. Lukeson had entered the room, Miranda Watts by the hand, the worse for wear, but smiling happily. She broke free and ran to Sarah Watts, whose icy composure dissolved in tears.

In the company of Assistant Chief Constable Alice Mulgrave, CS Frank 'Sermon' Doyle was as smug as a mouse who had discovered a cheese heaven. 'Never doubted that we'd come through with flying colours, ma'am,' he boasted. 'I had every confidence.' He smiled benignly at Lukeson, who thought: What a crock of proverbial. Lukeson, as expected, smiled back, but with a great deal less *bonhomie* than Doyle had shown. Mulgrave, wisely in Lukeson's opinion, dispensed with the horse manure and simply said: 'Well done, Sergeant. Please convey my congratulations to everyone involved.'

'I surely will, ma'am.'

'Now, I must be away,' Mulgrave said. 'Talk of more cuts,

I'm afraid.' She paused before she left. 'Would Tompkins have killed the girl, do you think?' she enquired of Lukeson.

'Desperate, she might have. Pity is, I don't think Linda Tompkins was that bad a person. She just got in way over her head, in her efforts to even a score with her sister.'

'Miranda Watts back safe and sound. The Swann murder solved. And the matter of Sally Swann sorted, too. Very impressive all round, Andy. Speckle would be chuffed,' It pleased Lukeson now that Mulrgave had departed and there was no reason for the spreading of horse manure, that Frank Doyle had expressed what he believed were genuine feelings. 'Pity about the Stockton business. Probably never get anyone for that now.'

Feeling weary and strangely despondent, when he should have been over the moon, Lukeson ignored the ringing phone when he entered his flat. When it rang again ten minutes later, and again half an hour later, he knew that ignoring it was not an option.

'Andy. . . .'

On hearing Sally Speckle his spirits zoomed.

'Like to come round?'

'Come round?'

'I've just put a casserole in the oven. It should be done by the time you get here.'

'You're back?'

'West Cork was nice, but it lacked something. What, I don't know.'

'It had Fergal,' he said, fishing.

'Fergal.' She laughed. 'You didn't think. . . ? Fergal Clancy is a friend from my Uni days. Graduated as an engineer. Went to Oz to work. Didn't like what he was doing. Gave in to his desire to be a painter, and ended up in West Cork trying to be Picasso while working as a deck-hand on a trawler to make ends meet.'

The red-haired, ruddy complexioned Fergal departed Andy Lukeson's mind. 'I'm on my way, Sally.'

'Fetch a bottle of ketchup on the way, will you?'

Ketchup.

He'd have fetched the moon, if she'd asked for it.

EPILOGUE

The man's foul breath was ragged now, soon the death rattles would begin. After three exhausting years as a hospital chaplain, the priest had reached the point where he could, more often than not, put a time on a dying person's final gasp. 'There was a girl, Father. . . .' The penitent's wheezing now sounded like nails being scraped across iron. A shadow crossed the bed. The priest looked up at the young doctor who had come to . . . do what? There was nothing anyone could do. 'He's making his peace with God,' he said. The doctor went to the nurses station to wait. '. . . Mischief done, Father. A young girl . . . a very young girl. A child. . . .' The dying man grabbed the priest's hand. 'An evil impulse, Father. I've always had this weakness, but only gave in to it one time.' The man closed his eyes, his face crimped in pain. 'Her name was Katherine, Father. Katherine Stockton. I would have, I think . . . But I never got the chance. She was found, before I could, you see,' he went on apace, desperate now to ready himself for judgement. 'Does that make me as guilty as if I had, Father?'

'God is a forgiving God,' said the elderly priest, as he had done a thousand times before.

'I was on my way to the police when I collapsed on the doorstep of the station.' Sweat was pouring from the man's every pore. The priest hoped that it would all be over soon for the man and, selfishly, for himself. For a priest, he had never been very good with death and the dying. He suddenly had a sense of coming to the end of his ministry. Over forty years a priest, he would welcome the rest. He imparted absolution, but the man was dead before he finished. The young doctor returned and went through the motions. Leaving the ward, the elderly priest decided that on the morrow he'd inform his superiors that he was retiring from ministry.

The next morning, he picked up a letter from the hall mat, opened it, read it. He put the letter in a drawer of the hall table. The letter noted that his superiors felt that he was of an age when a country parish might be more in keeping, and that from the first of the following month he would take up his new ministry in the Cotswolds. He went to the kitchen and filled out a bowl of cornflakes. Finished, he phoned the man who had signed the letter and told him that he was retiring. 'We will decide when you'll retire,' his superior intoned. He replaced the phone, put on his warm overcoat, and walked out of the parish house and the priesthood, feeling for the first time in a long time that God would, in His gentle way, choose for him the direction he would now take. At the corner newsagent he bought a newspaper which told the story of Miranda Watts safe return. Reading on, regret was expressed that Katherine Stockton's abductor could not

223

have also been brought to account. 'He has.' But he was, and would remain, the only person in the world who knew that.